Star of Wonder

JoAnn S. Dawson

Illustrated by Michelle Keenan

SOURCEBOOKS
Jabberwocky
AN IMPRINT OF SOURCEBOOKS

Published by Sourcebooks Jabberwocky, an imprint of Sourcebooks, Inc.
P.O. Box 4410, Naperville, Illinois 60567-4410
(630) 961-3900
Fax: (630) 961-2168
www.sourcebooks.com

Library of Congress Cataloging-in-Publication Data

Dawson, JoAnn.
   Star of Wonder / JoAnn Dawson.
      p. cm.
   Summary: When Mary's horse, Lady, gives birth to a baby on Christmas
eve, Mary and her best friend Jody name him Star, train him, and share
many adventures with him, as well as with Lady and the other animals on
the dairy farm where they board their horses.
   ISBN 978-1-4022-0997-0 (trade pbk.)
   [1. Horses--Fiction. 2. Domestic animals--Fiction. 3. Farm
life--Fiction.] I. Title.
   PZ7.D32735St 2007
   [Fic]--dc22
                                    2007027946

Printed and bound in the United States of America.
            VP 10 9 8 7 6 5 4 3 2 1

To Ted, Zach, and Nick
for all the love and joy

Lucky Foot Stable

Contents

✷ **1** ✷

Welcome

"YOU'RE RIGHT, JODY, Star of Wonder is the perfect name for him," Mary whispered as they gazed at the newborn foal sleeping peacefully in the straw. "Look, the star is exactly in the middle of his forehead, just like his father's. It even has five points, like a real star. And it's a wonder that he's here!"

"I know," replied Jody. "I still can't believe we didn't figure it out. Lady was getting so fat and grumpy and I didn't know why!"

Mary and Jody sat side by side on the thick bed of straw in Lady's stall at Lucky Foot Stable, in awe of the gift that had been given them on this cold clear Christmas morning. Colonel Sanders, the old white barn rooster, ruffled his feathers and peered down from his roost on the top board of Lady's stall while Gypsy Amber, Mary's pony, hung her head over the stall next door and nickered softly as if to say, "Welcome, Star of Wonder."

"Mary, look, under the stall door!" Jody giggled. "Poor Finnegan wants to come in and see what's happening!"

A black nose and two front paws were all that could be seen of Finnegan, the farm's herding dog, as he snuffled and scratched at the packed clay under the door.

"Maybe we should let him in," Mary said sympathetically. "After all, he is the one who woke us up to tell us about the baby!"

Mary and Jody were "epic friends," brought together by their love of their two ponies. They had camped out in the stable overnight on Christmas Eve, trying to stay awake until midnight to hear the animals speak, a legend that Mary had read about in one of her many books. But they had both fallen asleep just before the stroke of twelve, only to be awakened in the morning by Finnegan's whining and scratching at Lady's stall door. When Mary got up to investigate, she experienced the shock of her life at the completely unexpected sight of the black-and-white foal struggling to stand on his spindly legs as Lady, his proud mother, gently licked the top of his head.

"OK, Finnegan, you can come in if you promise to be quiet and calm and not wake the baby!" Mary giggled, carefully opening the stall door. Finnegan's whole body wagged as he entered the stall, but upon seeing the sleeping foal, he stopped in his tracks, pricked up his ears, and cocked his head as if to say, "What in the world is that?" Mary and Jody covered their mouths to keep from laughing out loud at the look on the dog's face.

"Finney, meet Star of Wonder. We know you weren't expecting him, and neither were we, but he's here and we're going to help Lady take care of him," Mary explained.

Lady snorted and pinned her ears back at the sight of the intruder, and Finnegan took a step back, not sure what to do.

"Lady, it's all right—you know Finnegan! He's not going to hurt Star. He just wants to see him," Jody said, petting the hapless dog to show Lady that he was no threat. Lady shook her head up and down and extended her nose for Finnegan to sniff, and they were friends again.

"Mary, I just thought of something!" Jody exclaimed. "I don't know what time it is, but I bet it's almost milking time. We've got to get Willie!"

Willie was the old cowhand on Mr. McMurray's dairy farm where Jody and Mary kept the ponies. While he spent most of his time taking care of the cows, he sometimes helped the girls with the ponies—like the time that past spring when he hauled Lady to a horse show in the back of his old red pickup truck. The girls were now gazing at the result of that trip, when Lady had gotten herself into a paddock with a beautiful black stallion.

"You're right, Jode. I'll go see if he's here yet!" Mary started to jump up in her usual way, but remembering to be quiet around the foal, she raised herself gently from the straw. Before she reached the stall door, she was greeted by a familiar voice.

"Well, what in tarnation do we have here?" Willie said, looking through the open door and tugging on his earlobe.

"Willie! I was just coming to get you! It's a foal! Lady had a baby! We didn't even know! We fell asleep before midnight, and Finney woke us up this morning, and here he was in the stall!" Mary exclaimed all in one breath.

"Hmph," Willie said, taking off his hat and scratching the side of his head.

"Willie, is that all you have to say? Isn't it a miracle?" Jody whispered.

"A miracle? I don't know about that," Willie smiled. "I reckon I can figure out how it happened."

"Oh, Willie, we did figure out how it happened. I mean, we knew Lady was in the paddock with the stallion at the horse show, but we just never thought about it—even when Lady was getting all fat and lazy!" Jody continued.

"Willie, you don't even look surprised!" Mary said suspiciously. "Willie—you knew all along, didn't you? You knew and you didn't tell us!"

"Hmph," Willie replied with a hint of a smile playing on his lips.

"Well, if you wanted us to be surprised, you did a good job!" Jody cried. "We were surprised, all right!"

"Now, who do you think has been givin' that old plug extra grain and makin' sure she was gettin' all the hay she needed to make sure that baby was growin' the way it should in her belly?" Willie asked.

Normally Jody would be offended at Willie calling Lady an "old plug," but she was still trying to absorb the fact that Willie had known about Star all along.

"Willie, guess what we named him?" Mary said, forgetting to be mad at Willie for keeping such a big secret.

"You named him already?"

"Of course, we've been in here with him for an hour!" Mary exclaimed. "When we were trying to stay awake last night to hear the animals talk, we decided to sing Christmas carols, and the one we knew the words to was 'We Three Kings.' So we sang it, and the chorus goes, 'Star of wonder, star of night, star with royal beauty bright.' So since he has that perfect bright star, and he's such a wonder, we named him Star of Wonder—Star for short. And it was all Jody's idea," she continued generously.

Just as if Star of Wonder had heard his name called, he raised his head from the straw and blinked, first at Mary, then at Jody, and finally at Willie before raising himself to a more upright position. He blinked again, shook his head, and blew through his nose. Then, just as Lady had done, he stretched his neck and offered his muzzle for Finnegan to sniff.

"He's a right cheeky thing, ain't he?" Willie chuckled.

"Look, he's trying to get up again!" Jody giggled.

The gangly foal stretched out his front legs in the straw and raised himself up as far as he could, trying to push off with his hindquarters. Wobbling to and fro, he managed to get his rear end off the ground just long enough to lose his balance and flop back down on his side.

"You girls move out of the way and give him some more room," Willie instructed. "He may look small, but if he lands on you, you're gonna know it."

"But Willie, can't we help him? If Jody gets on one side and me on the other, we could help him up!" Mary exclaimed.

"You just let him get up on his own," Willie said. "He'll get it in a minute. He already knows how to stand, he's just got to figure it out."

So Mary and Jody backed up against the stall boards while the determined foal tried once again to get his impossibly fragile legs under him. As he rocked back and forth, Lady nickered her encouragement and nuzzled him gently until he finally stood, legs splayed but sturdy enough to help him stay up. Now he only had to turn himself around far enough to get his muzzle under Lady's belly where the nourishing first milk was. As if she knew he would have

The gangly foal stretched out his front legs in the straw and raised himself up as far as he could.

difficulty with that maneuver, Lady turned her own body around to accommodate him.

"He's already nursed once, Willie. We watched him." Mary said.

"I see he's got the stallion's black color but Lady's white patches across his withers. And look at those white stockings all the way up to his knees and hocks. He's gonna be a real looker," Willie said admiringly.

The foal felt along Lady's side with his muzzle, pushing and snuffling, trying to find the right spot, but he couldn't quite remember where he had nursed only an hour before.

"Oh, Willie, can't we help him now? He just needs a little guidance," Jody implored.

"Well, I reckon it couldn't hurt. Just push his head down a little and guide his mouth up to her udder, and then he'll get the picture."

The girls almost ran into each other in their eagerness to help the foal find Lady's milk. Mary stood back in deference to the fact that Lady was Jody's pony but braced herself against Star's body to help him stand while Jody guided his muzzle low enough to find Lady's udder, swollen with milk. Then all was quiet except for the sounds of suckling as the foal took to his task with enthusiasm. Willie, watching silently from the stall door, suddenly turned away.

"Well, I've had enough of this foolishness," he said gruffly, rubbing his gnarly hand across his eyes. "Got to get to the barn. It'll be milkin' time before you know it."

A Dangerous Lesson

S TAR OF WONDER'S birth turned out to be quite an event at Lucky Foot Stable. Even Mr. McMurray, the owner of the dairy farm where the little green-roofed stable sat next to the huge cow barn—biggest one in the county, Willie often said—came by later that week to welcome the baby into the world. Mary and Jody were just taking down the little Christmas tree from the top of Jody's tack box when he appeared in the doorway.

"Well, girls, I hear congratulations are in order,"

he said in his thick Irish brogue. "You know, I don't care so much for horses, hay burners they are, and eating the cow's pasture for no profit, but I would like to see the little devil. Willie says he's right smart looking."

Mary finally found her voice after the initial surprise of seeing Mr. McMurray in Lucky Foot Stable, where he had rarely set foot since the day he agreed to let the girls keep the ponies there in exchange for carpentry work from Jody's father and bookkeeping from Mary's mother.

"Oh, yes, sir. He is, and right smart in the head too!" she exclaimed proudly. "We've already put a halter on him, and he didn't care a bit!"

"Come see him—he's out in the paddock with Lady," Jody said, forgetting her shyness and taking a surprised Mr. McMurray by the hand.

The snow that had fallen lightly on Christmas Eve still remained in small patches here and there in the paddock, and Star of Wonder was pawing and snuffling at one of these curious white spots when Mr. McMurray looked over the door of the stable into the paddock. As soon as the foal saw the new face, he stopped pawing and boldly walked over, raised his muzzle, and sniffed Mr. McMurray's outstretched hand.

"He's not shy, now, is he?" Mr. McMurray said, chuckling as he rubbed the top of Star's head. Lady raised her head for a moment from her pile of hay, but anticipating no danger from this visitor, quickly resumed her breakfast.

"He's getting really strong and loves to run around," Jody said. As if on cue, Star flung up his head and spun in a circle, prancing and kicking across the paddock on his spindly legs. Mr. McMurray laughed out loud at his antics as the girls watched him with pride.

"Well, girls, like I said, I never had much use for horses, but I will say he is a handsome lad, and full of the devil!" He laughed as Star took another turn around the paddock, bucking and kicking up his heels.

"Mr. McMurray, Christmas break is almost over and next week we have to go back to school," Mary spoke up. "We're a little worried about Star because he needs us."

"He needs you, does he?" Mr. McMurray said. "And what about his mama? Doesn't she take good care of him?"

"Well, yes, but Lady needs us too. She has to be fed extra grain so she can make good milk, and we have to turn her out at separate times from Gypsy for right now until the baby gets a little bigger, and somebody needs to keep an eye on Star because he runs around like crazy, and we're afraid he's going to fall down and break his leg!" Mary continued breathlessly.

"Hmm, I see—so what are you saying, Mary?" Mr. McMurray asked.

"Well, I just wondered, since you came to see him and everything, and you think he's a right smart handsome lad, if you could just look in on him once in a while. And maybe you wouldn't mind if Willie came over when he's not too busy with the cows to turn out Lady and Star and bring in Gypsy during the day?"

"And I'll be here after school, as soon as I finish my homework," Jody added. "My dad got me a new bike for Christmas and I can get here really fast from my house!"

"And instead of going home from school and then riding my bike here, my mom said she could pick me up from school and bring me straight here, as long as I get back home in time to do my homework before bed!" Mary said.

Mr. McMurray looked from one girl's upturned face to the other and tried to sound serious.

"I'll have a word with Willie and see what we can do," he said. "But we can't take too much time away from the cows, you know."

"Oh, we know, sir, and we'll help Willie with them too, if he needs it." Jody promised. "And as soon as Star gets bigger and gets weaned, and it gets to be spring, we won't worry so much. Because the ponies will be out in the pasture all the time."

"Am I interrupting anything?" a voice came from the stable aisle.

"Mom!" Mary said, turning to see her mother, who was dressed in her best work clothes. "I was just talking about you!"

"I thought I would stop on my way to work and check up on that new baby," Mary's mother said, looking out over the stable door. "Hello, Jody. And Mr. McMurray. How are you today?"

"I'm well, Mrs. Morrow. I think that's a fine looking colt out there, and the girls are thrilled, of course."

"Oh, yes, and he's grown since just a few days ago!" she exclaimed. Mary was pleasantly surprised to see her mother in the stable, because her mother didn't like the smell of horse manure, and the high heels she wore to work weren't suited to walking in a barn.

"Mom, I was just telling Mr. McMurray that maybe you could pick me up at school and get me here fast so I can help Jody take care of Lady and Star," Mary said hopefully.

"I'm going to try, Mary, but you know some days I won't be able to take a break from work. And what about your schoolwork?"

"I'll be home in time to do it before I go to bed. Mom, I've been getting straight As, remember?"

Mrs. Morrow smiled and shook her head. Ever since Mary's father had left the family when Mary was a baby, her mother had worked hard to keep them together and happy. But sometimes she wondered why the two of them were so unlike each other. Almost since Mary could talk, she had asked for a pony every year for Christmas, and her room was filled with horse books, horse posters, horse calendars, and horse models. Mrs. Morrow had finally decided that Mary was ready for a real horse, and so they found the dark chestnut pony with the flaxen mane and tail at a horse and pony rescue stable. Mary named the mare Gypsy Amber, and she made up a suitably wild story to explain her background, although Mary's mother knew that the pony had come from a home where she had been neglected to the point of starvation. Mrs. Morrow had contacted Mr. McMurray about using a stall in the little white and green stable in return for developing a good record-keeping system for his cows and monthly bookkeeping. And Jody had arrived a month later with her little pinto Lady. The girls had been inseparable ever since, and Mrs. Morrow never regretted her decision.

"Well, I've got to get to work." Mrs. Morrow said, stepping gingerly across the dirt floor of the stable aisle, balancing on her toes. "I'll see you at home later, Mary, and don't forget . . ."

"I know, I know, take my barn clothes off on the porch before coming in the house," Mary recited with a smile.

After all visitors had departed from Lucky Foot Stable, Mary and Jody decided to give Star a lesson in being led around the paddock. "Star was so good when we put the halter on him—he shouldn't mind the lead rope at all," Mary said confidently. Lady's halter was obviously too big, so Willie had given the girls an old calf halter for the foal and it fit him perfectly. Now it was time to fasten the lead rope to it and teach Star to lead.

*He kicked and bucked around the paddock once with his
tail held high and his back toward the girls.*

"Mare, are you sure we're not pushing him? He's only a week old, you know," Jody worried.

"Well, we've been petting him and rubbing him and we even brushed him, and he loved that," Mary said. "And he already follows us around like a dog, so what's the difference if we have a rope on him?"

The difference was clear the instant Jody snapped the rope onto Star's halter and gave a little tug. Star was fine following Jody and Mary of his own free will, but when he felt the pressure on his head to go forward, he automatically pulled back and threw up his head, yanking the lead rope from Jody's hand and taking off at a canter across the paddock.

"Star!" Mary shrieked. "Jody, the rope is hanging down between his legs! It could wrap around them and trip him! He'll break his leg!"

Mary and Jody both knew that chasing the foal would be the worst thing they could do—he would just run faster. As it was, he kicked and bucked around the paddock once, then he trotted, with his tail high and his back toward the girls, sidestepping away from them at the last minute. Just as he went by, Mary reached out to grab the rope, but she missed. Jody was almost crying as she watched the rope flip in and out between Star's fragile front legs.

Lady, meanwhile, looked up from her hay just as the foal trotted past. Until then, Lady had paid little attention to Star galloping around the paddock. But as he trotted near her, she seemed to almost know that the dangling rope was dangerous and reached out and grabbed it in her teeth, stopping Star in his tracks.

Mary and Jody stared in amazement as Lady stood calmly holding the end of the rope in her teeth while Star rubbed his muzzle on her neck, then moved down her flank and nuzzled for milk. The girls turned and looked at each other and burst out laughing at the same instant.

"I can't believe she did that!" Jody gasped. "We have to tell Willie!"

"Willie will never believe it," Mary replied. "I wish we had a camera, just so we could prove it!"

"Well, I guess we pushed him a little too fast," Jody giggled. "Let's unhook him and try again in about six months."

$\star$ 3 $\star$

Time to Grow Up

BY THE TIME six months had passed, not only had Star learned to lead around the paddock, but Mary and Jody had led him around the whole farm, introducing him to the cows, taking him to see Willie out in the field, even walking him up to Mr. McMurray's big stone house. Of course, they led Lady along with him, because Star was still dependent on her milk and her company. They had even placed a saddle on his back and tightened the girth one hole at a time until he got used to the feel of it, and they laughed to see his expression when he turned to look at the funny thing. They had begun to feed him small amounts of grain, and he had started to nibble on Lady's hay. It was summer, and the time had come for Willie to give the girls some advice on the next step in Star's upbringing. Ever since the day Willie had challenged the stallion at the horse show, the girls had realized that he knew much more about horses than they had ever suspected.

"You know, it's time for him to grow up a little more," Willie said to the girls as they led Star around the paddock with Lady's saddle on his back.

"What do you mean, Willie?" asked Mary. "He's growing every day. Look how big he's getting!"

"I mean, he's got to grow up in his head. He's got to get away from bein' so attached to Lady."

"But, Willie, he's only six months old," Jody said. "He's still nursing!"

"I know he's still nursin',' but it's high time he quit nursin' and started eatin' on his own. Lady's milk won't last forever, you know," Willie replied, tugging on his earlobe.

"Well, he has been eating on his own—he eats grain now, and a little hay, and he drinks water sometimes. He'll stop nursing pretty soon," Mary commented matter-of-factly.

"But, Mary, he's got to be weaned. I know you know what that word means, with all the horse books you have and that dictionary you're always looking things up in," Willie insisted.

Mary stared at Willie speechlessly, until Jody interrupted the silence with a question.

"Mare, what does he mean?"

"Well, it means we have to separate Star from Lady, so her milk will dry up, and he'll have to eat just grain and hay and drink water from now on." Mary explained solemnly.

"Separate them? But they'll both go crazy! Remember that time Lady got stuck in the stable somehow while Star was in the paddock, and she almost broke the door down trying to get to him?!" Jody cried.

"He was a lot younger then," Willie said. "Now he's older and even Lady knows he should be on his own. Haven't you seen her pushin' him away sometimes when he comes to nurse?"

The girls looked at each other in silence, knowing it was true but not wanting to admit it.

"But, Willie, what should we do? Do you have any ideas?" Jody asked.

"Well," Willie said, taking off his hat and scratching his head like he always did when he was thinking,

"I reckon we could put Lady and Gypsy together out in the pasture like we always used to, and keep Star here in the paddock. You girls will have to keep him company until he gets used to the idea of not being with Lady."

"But he's going to run around and cry like he did the day Lady was stuck in the stable," Jody said, feeling like crying herself.

"He will; I won't lie to you," Willie said, "and Lady will be upset too, even though she's gettin' tired of him nursin' on her. I wish there was a place we could put Lady far enough away where they couldn't hear each other hollerin,' but the cow pasture's as far as she can go.

"It's got to be done. They'll be all right in a month or so, and then they can go back together again after Lady's milk dries up, and they won't be so attached to each other. And Jody'll be able to ride Lady again without Star trailin' along."

Mary and Jody looked at Star, who blinked at them with so much trust in his eyes, and at Lady, who was nibbling on her hay at the other end of the paddock. Jody sighed and then looked at Willie.

"When should we start?" she asked in resignation.

"Well, no sense puttin' it off," Willie said. "Today's as good a day as any."

"Today?" Mary cried. "But, Willie, we haven't even had a chance to get used to the idea!"

"No point in waitin' for that. You might never get used to it. You just have to do it. Now, Jody, get that saddle off Star and give me his lead rope. I don't want you tryin' to hold onto him when he starts runnin' around. In fact, I want you both in the stable, not out in the paddock with him. I'll get Lady and take her around to the pasture. Gypsy's out there, ain't she, Mary?"

Mary was almost too upset to reply. "Yes, she's out there, Willie. She'll be glad to see Lady. But, Willie, are you sure we have to do this today?"

Willie was already halfway across the paddock with the lead rope, and Jody had already taken the saddle off. The girls obediently went into the stable, looking out into the paddock from the stable door.

Willie hooked the lead rope to Lady's halter and walked her toward the gate. Star was at her side in an instant, expecting to go out of the gate with her as he had done so many times before on their trips around the farm with the girls. But this time, Willie hurried out with Lady and turned, shutting the gate before Star could follow.

"Oh, I can't stand it," Jody said, covering her eyes.

"I'll be back in a minute," Willie called to the girls. "Don't do anything until I get back. And stay in that stable."

The experience of watching Lady walk away from him was a first for Star; he had always been by her side. He threw up his head in surprise, then turned and looked at Mary and Jody, as if to say, "Hey! Get over here and open this gate!"

But Mary and Jody, as much as they wanted to go out in the paddock, stayed where they were. Star stood stock-still, head up and staring as Lady and Willie turned the corner of the dairy barn on the way to the big pasture. The moment Lady was out of sight, Star shook his head, snorted once, and let out a high-pitched whinny. An instant later, Lady answered from the pasture.

"I was hoping he wouldn't be able to hear Lady from the pasture, but he can hear her loud and clear," Mary lamented. "This is going to be terrible!"

Star whinnied again, Lady answered, then Star began galloping around the paddock, kicking and bucking, stopping only long enough to whinny once again, then taking off for another round.

"Mary, he's going to either run himself to death or hurt himself trying. I'm going out there to try and calm him down," Jody said, pushing open the stable door.

"Don't you do no such thing," Willie said. He had come silently into the stable and was watching Star from the aisle behind the girls.

"But, Willie, he's going to break a leg!" Mary cried.

"No, he's not. His legs are a lot sturdier than you think they are. He'll run around until he gets tired, then he'll stop," Willie said simply.

Mary and Willie continued to watch Star gallop and whinny, but Jody sat on a bale of hay in the stable with her eyes closed and her hands over her ears. She suddenly felt a warm wet tongue on her face. Finnegan had come into the stable to see what all the commotion was about and was doing his best to cheer her up.

"Oh, Finney," Jody cried, throwing her arms around him and burying her face in his fur. "I can't watch. When is it going to stop?"

As if on cue, the whinnying did stop, and so did the sound of hooves beating against the hard clay of the paddock. Jody sat up on her bale and looked at Mary and Willie, who still had their backs to her as they stared out into the paddock.

"What's happening?" Jody asked fearfully. "Is he all right?"

"Just like I told you. He'd run till he got tired, and then he'd stop," Willie replied calmly.

"Jode, I don't think you want to see him right now." Mary warned, "Better wait a few minutes."

Of course, that statement made Jody jump from her bale and rush to the door. What she saw across the paddock brought tears to her eyes.

Poor Star had run himself into a lather, and he was standing by the gate, head hanging to the ground. Having no more voice left, he made snuffling noises that sounded to Jody like crying. And she began to cry herself.

"Oh, Willie, what have we done to him? He'll never forgive us," Jody wailed.

"Oh, yes, he will," said Willie, patting Jody awkwardly on the back. "You go on out there to him now and give him a pat. He's missin' his mama, but he'll be better tomorrow. See if he wants a drink, but just give him a little until he cools down."

Jody wiped her eyes and started off across the paddock to Star. Mary was close behind, but Willie caught her by the arm before she went very far.

"Let Jody go to him, Mary," Willie said. "He needs to make a connection with somebody besides Lady, but just one person for now. He's feelin' pretty blue."

As much as she wanted to be with Star, Mary stopped and nodded. She watched silently as Jody approached Star with an outstretched hand.

"Star, I'm so sorry," Jody said quietly. Star's breathing had slowed down, and when he saw Jody's familiar figure, he raised his head, blinked at her as he always did, and stretched out his muzzle to sniff her hand. Jody turned and smiled at Mary and Willie.

"I think he still likes me," she said. Star sighed, took a step closer to Jody, and laid his head wearily on her arm, nickering softly.

"Willie, can I take out a little water in a bucket for him now?" Mary whispered. "I won't bother him, I promise."

"I reckon that'd be alright," Willie said.

Mary took the water out in a small bucket and held it under Star's muzzle. He sniffed the water, but didn't drink. Instead he began rubbing his head up and down, up and down on Jody's arm like he always

"Come on, Star," Mary said quietly. *"I know you're thirsty, boy, and you've cooled down enough now."*

did when he had an itch.

"Come on, Star," Mary said quietly. "I know you're thirsty, boy, and you've cooled down enough now to drink a little bit."

Star finished rubbing Jody's arm and sniffed the water again, tentatively lapping at it with his tongue like a dog before taking a real drink.

"That's a good boy," Jody said. "I know it's not as good as Lady's milk, but you've got to get used to it."

"Don't say anything to remind him of Lady," Mary whispered. "He's got to forget about her for a while. Let's see if he'll eat some grain."

The girls walked slowly toward the stable to get the grain, hoping Star would follow them in his usual way. Star stood still for a moment, watching them go, and then, on tired unsteady legs, he trailed after them to the stable door. Mary went in to get the grain while Jody stayed with Star outside the stable. Willie reached over the door and rubbed Star's head briskly between the ears.

"Feelin' sorry for yourself, ain't you, buddy?" he asked sympathetically. "You'll have a sorry night tonight, but you'll feel a little better tomorrow."

Just then another long, plaintive whinny came from the direction of the big pasture, and Star again threw up his head and tried to whinny back, but a hoarse squeal was all that he could muster. He shook his head in frustration as Mary came out with the scoop of grain and offered him a bite. He shook his head again, reached out, got his nose under the scoop, and flipped it right out of Mary's hand, scattering grain all over the ground.

"Star! Where are your manners?" Jody cried.

"He's startin' to get his strength back, and rememberin' how ornery he can be," Willie laughed as Star turned and cantered across the paddock, throwing in a buck for good measure. Then he turned and trotted back to the girls, dropped his head, and began lipping at the grain, picking up one piece at a time from the packed clay of the paddock.

"See, he's forgettin' about his mama already. Ain't that always the way?" Willie said. "He's gonna be fine, just like I told you."

"But, Willie, we can't leave him alone tonight," Jody worried. "We'll have to stay here and sleep in the stable. Should we put him in Lady's stall? We could sleep right next door in Gypsy's, in case he needs us."

"What's all this about sleeping in a barn?" asked a familiar voice from somewhere behind Willie.

"Dad!" Jody cried, as her father stuck his head over

the stable door. "What are you doing here?"

"Well, I'm glad you're happy to see me," he chuckled. "How are you, Willie?"

"No use complainin', Frank," Willie replied. "Are you workin' on a project?"

"I stopped by to help Mr. McMurray hang that new sliding door on the cow stable, and I thought I'd come over and see how the little guy is doing. He doesn't look too happy. And where's Lady?"

"Oh, Dad, we had to wean him today. He's *not* very happy, and he ran around and around and got all sweaty, and he kept calling to Lady, and she called back, and now he's settled down a little, but we don't think we should leave him alone tonight because he's going to need some company, so can I stay here with Mary overnight? Please? Please?"

"Well, I'll have to think about that," Mr. Stafford replied. "Did Mary's mother say it was all right?"

"Um, well, not exactly, not yet anyway, but I'm going to call her at work and ask," Mary said quickly. "I don't think she'll mind, as long as Finnegan's here to protect us!"

Jody's father looked from one girl to the other, trying to look stern. Since the day three years ago when Jody's mother had passed away, he had made all the decisions about her upbringing alone, and he knew that having Lady in her life was the key that lifted Jody's spirits the most and helped her through that dark time in both their lives. And when Jody met Mary, Mr. Stafford was so thankful that he rarely refused Jody anything having to do with her "epic friend." As he looked at the girls' pleading faces, he knew this was one of those times.

"Well, I guess it can't hurt. What do you think, Willie?"

Willie took off his cap and scratched the side of his head. "I reckon they can't get into too much mischief. And the little fella does need some company on his first night without his mama . . ."

Before Willie could finish his sentence, Jody was hugging her dad and Mary was jumping up and down. "Thanks ever so, Mr. Stafford, and Willie, if we get into any mischief, you can make us clean out the calf stalls."

"Now, that's not a bad idea," Willie replied, "but right now you two better go see about Lady. She's havin' a hard time too, you know."

"Oh, my gosh, I was so busy worrying about Star that I didn't think too much about Lady," Jody said regretfully.

"Let's get some sugar cubes! That might take her mind off him," Mary offered.

Before Willie could say another word, the girls were off to the big pasture with sugar cubes in hand. Rounding the corner of the dairy barn, they moaned in dismay at the sight of poor Lady, who was galloping to the end of the fence line and back again, stopping only to attempt a raspy whinny from her worn-out throat. Gypsy stood by the gate, helplessly watching her pasture mate.

"Oh, Lady, here we are! We've got something for you!" Jody cried, running to open the gate.

"Your favorite—sugar cubes! Come on, girl."

At the familiar sound of Jody's voice, Lady stopped in her tracks at the far end of the fence line and flung up her head, nostrils flaring. She attempted another whinny, then came straight at the girls with a high stepping trot, her tail flowing behind her like one of the wild Arabians in Mary's books. She halted just short of Jody's outstretched hand and extended her muzzle to sniff the sugar. But for once, Lady was not interested in the treat. Just as Star had done with the scoop of grain, Lady knocked the cube from Jody's hand and began pushing Jody toward the gate with her head.

"Look, she wants you to open the gate and let her

out so she can get back to Star," Mary giggled.

"Mare, it's not funny. I feel so bad for her. What should we do?"

"There's nothing we can do. Willie said she'll be better tomorrow. We just have to be patient," Mary replied. "Gypsy! You keep Lady company and try to make her feel better!" she continued. But Gypsy, not having a clue what was the matter with Lady, instead dropped her head to graze.

"Come on, Jody. We'll just have to let her be miserable. We can visit her later when it gets dark and make sure she's okay. We'd better get back to Star. And we have to get the stable ready for our sleepover!"

4

A Sleepless Night

BY THE TIME Mary and Jody finished making a bed of straw for themselves in the corner of Lucky Foot Stable, Star had settled down in the stall he had shared with Lady and was listlessly nipping at the mound of hay the girls had put there to get his mind off the taste of his mother's milk. Finnegan was testing out the girls' bed by rolling back and forth in it, and Colonel Sanders was perched on his roost on the top board of the stall, ruffling his feathers and settling in for the night. His old white head had just started to nod in sleep when Star crept silently over, and with one swift motion, stuck his muzzle under the rooster's tail feathers, and pushed. Poor Colonel Sanders squawked in surprise and was able to flap his wings just in time to help him land on his feet instead of his head on the dirt floor of the stable.

"Star!" Jody admonished the mischievous colt. "What are you doing? Just because you're missing Lady doesn't give you an excuse to forget your manners! Poor Colonel Sanders!" she continued, trying not to laugh at the sight of the flustered rooster, shaking his head and flapping his wings in an effort to regain his dignity.

"Jody, you've got to stop reminding him of Lady. We have to promise to not even say her name again tonight, or ever, until he forgets about her. Willie said it might take a whole month!"

"Willie also said that he'll be able to smell Lady's scent on our clothes, so it won't matter if we say her name or not. Every time we visit her and then see him, he'll be reminded of her.

Don't you remember when we came back to the paddock today? He had a fit!"

And it was true. At the sight of the girls rounding the corner of the barn that afternoon, Star had simply nickered quietly at the gate, but when they came close enough for him to sniff, he threw up his head and started another round of whinnying and galloping around the paddock. Lady wasted no time in answering, and the desperate scene from earlier in the day was repeated.

The girls had finally succeeded in quieting him down enough to lead him into the stall, where they petted and brushed him and gave him sugar cubes to distract him from his misery.

Now it was dark and time for bed, and the girls brought their sleeping bags down from the loft and spread them on the straw.

"I'm glad we kept these here from Christmas Eve," Mary said gratefully. "It would be really scratchy to sleep right on top of the straw."

"Mare, we said we were going to visit Lady before we went to sleep. Should we?"

"No, because if Star catches a whiff of her on us, he'll just start up again. Look, he's pretty much settled down after his mischief with Colonel Sanders. Maybe he took his last frustrations out on him for the night."

"I know what we should do! Tomorrow," suggested Jody, "we'll have to go home and get two sets of clothes—one for visiting Lady and one for being with Star. And we'll have to wash our hands really well every time we get finished with Lady. That way he won't be able to smell her."

"Grand idea!" Mary agreed. "Now, we need to get to sleep so we can wake up early and take him for a walk."

So the girls went one last time into Star's stall and patted and stroked and cooed over him until they were sure he was feeling quite comforted. Colonel Sanders had adjusted his roosting place to the top board of Gypsy's stall, and after Mary removed Finnegan from the middle of her sleeping bag to a position between the two bags, the girls were ready to sleep.

"Nice to have Finney here to protect us," Mary yawned.

"I'm glad we don't have to try and stay up until midnight tonight to hear the animals talk," Jody said sleepily, remembering their failed attempt on Christmas Eve. "Worrying about Star all day has worn me out."

"Hmmmm" Mary murmured, closing her eyes and snuggling against Finnegan.

The girls were just drifting off to sleep when a small scratching sound coming from the corner of the stable caught Finnegan's attention. He raised his head and pricked up his ears, sniffing the air curiously. The sound stopped, then came again. Now Finnegan, fully alert, whined and stood up, his paw landing squarely in the middle of Mary's stomach.

"Finnegan!" Mary whispered drowsily, "what's the matter with you? There are no foals being born tonight. Go back to sleep."

But the inquisitive dog was already halfway across the stable in a half-crouch position, head low and sniffing the ground as he stalked closer to the object of his curiosity.

Jody turned over in her sleeping bag and squinted into the gloom, which was only dimly illuminated by a sliver of cloud-covered moonlight through the dusty window of the stable.

"What's going on?" she asked. "What's Finney doing?"

"I don't know. He sees something. Listen . . . do you hear that?"

The scratching noise came again, louder this time. As Finnegan drew closer to the sound, the girls propped themselves up on their elbows and strained their eyes into the shadows.

At that moment, the moonlight became brighter as the cloud passed over, and the girls saw the object

Mary and Jody screamed and jumped up from their sleeping bags.

of Finnegan's attention—a large brown rat chewing and scratching busily in an attempt to gain entry into a bag of horse feed resting in the corner. The intruder was too absorbed in his task to notice the crafty dog stalking him. Before the girls could move, Finnegan pounced, taking the astonished rat in his jaws. The rat squealed in terror, Mary and Jody screamed in unison and jumped from their sleeping bags, and Star whinnied from his stall at the uproar.

Finnegan shook his prey furiously back and forth and squeezed with his teeth until the rat was silent and hung still and lifeless in his jaws. Then, dropping the unfortunate animal at the girls' feet, he sat down and wagged his tail proudly, waiting to be praised for his rat-killing prowess.

"Finnegan!" cried Jody. "What did you do that for?"

"Don't yell at him, Jody!" Mary said. "He thinks he's just doing his job. And he is, really. He kept that rat out of the pony's grain, and we should thank him for it."

But before the girls could give Finnegan a good pat on the head, a distant whinny came from the direction of the big pasture. Star flung up his head, spun around in his stall, and answered back.

"Oh, no, not again," Mary lamented. "I was hoping

Star was settled down for the night! I bet when he heard the rat squeal, it sounded like a whinny and that's why he whinnied back. Then Lady must have heard him. Now they'll go on forever, and we'll be up all night!"

But Star and Lady didn't go on all night. They only called to each other a few more times. Star stomped his foot and shook his head in frustration, but he quieted down after Jody gave him a handful of grain and scratched him on the special spot at the top of his withers that Willie had shown her.

No, it wasn't whinnying that kept the girls up all night—it was the hooting of the barn owls, the scurrying of the squirrels on the stable roof, the curious screams of a fox in the distance, the intermittent moos of a lonely calf, and the occasional menacing growls of Finnegan as he stared out the stable door at nothing in particular. Mary and Jody spent most of the night sitting up in their sleeping bags with their arms linked, asking each other, "What was that?" every five minutes. By the time they finally laid down in exhaustion, the sun was beginning to peek through the dusty windows of Lucky Foot Stable.

★ 5 ★

Lady's Tears

SUNLIGHT WAS STREAMING into Lucky Foot
Stable later that morning when Willie finished
the milking and hobbled silently in to check on
Mary and Jody. Even Finnegan's yip of greeting and
Star's nicker as Willie entered the stable door didn't
awaken the sleeping girls, as exhausted as they were
from their night of adventure. Willie stood for a
moment, looking from the girl's still forms to the
lifeless rat on the clay floor to Star pacing restlessly
in his stall. Finnegan followed as Willie walked over
and spoke softly to the handsome colt.

"Well, I reckon it's time to turn you out, fella, and it looks like these girls ain't ready to get up and do it," he said. "Come on, then, out in the paddock you go, and no hollerin' this mornin.' I'll get you some hay and a little grain, and you best be quiet."

So out in the paddock he went, and he was quiet, eating his grain with more enthusiasm than the day before and taking a long drink of the water Willie offered him.

"You'll be all right in a week or two," Willie said kindly, scratching Star on the special spot high on his shoulder. "Now finish the grain, and then that hay should keep you busy 'til the girls wake up. Come on, dog, time to round up the heifers."

But the girls didn't wake up until the sun had risen high enough to cast a beam of light directly onto Mary's face, causing her to try and brush away the heat with her hand. She turned drowsily on her side and slowly opened her eyes.

"Aaaagghh!" she screeched, as the first sight to greet her was the bloody dead rat, lying about a foot from her head.

"What is the matter with you?" Jody cried, rolling over and adding her own screech to Mary's when she spied the rat. The girls turned and looked at each other and burst out laughing at the same instant.

"We've got to get rid of that thing," Jody said with a grimace. "Maybe we should get Willie."

"Nonsense!" Mary replied bravely. "It's dead, and it can't bite. Out the window it goes!"

And she picked up the rat by the tail, carried it gingerly to the open window, and threw it out into the paddock.

"Mare! You can't just throw it out there! We've got to bury it, or it will smell up the whole stable! And Star won't want to share his paddock with a dead rat. Will you, Staa . . ."

Jody jumped up from her sleeping bag before she could finish her sentence, and Mary followed her gaze to the empty stall where Star was supposed to be.

"Star?" Mary said to the vacant space. "Star?" she repeated. "Where are you?"

"Oh, no, he must've broken out of his stall and ran out . . ."

". . . the back of the stable and out to the pasture to be with Lady!" Mary finished Jody's sentence as they both tore out of the stable and ran toward the big pasture in pursuit of Star, who all the while was munching contentedly on his hay in the paddock with the dead rat for company.

In one frantic glance as they rounded the corner of the big white dairy barn, the girls saw Willie opening the gate of the pasture, Gypsy grazing under the weeping willow tree, a cow and her newborn calf in the middle of the pasture, and Lady standing near the cow, stomping her foot and shaking her head up and down in agitation. But they didn't see Star anywhere.

"Willie!" Mary yelled breathlessly as she and Jody squeezed through the gate after him. "Have you seen Star? Is he out here? He's not in the stable! He got out of his stall somehow and we can't find him anywhere!"

Willie turned to Mary impatiently. "What the . . . got out of his stall?" he replied testily. "Can't find him anywhere? Well, you didn't look too hard, did ya?" And he kept walking toward the newborn calf.

"Willie!" Jody insisted, following close behind. "What do you mean? He's not in his stall, and he's not out here . . . where else could he be?"

"He's right where he's s'posed to be—out in the paddock, where he shoulda been first thing this mornin' if you two lazybones hadn'ta slept so late. Now, don't bother me, I got to get your old plug Lady away from that calf—she's actin' crazy."

Mary and Jody looked at each other in disbelief. "We never even looked in the paddock!" Mary cried, and then realized what Willie had just said. "What do you mean, Willie? Who's acting crazy?"

Willie turned again and almost tripped over the two girls. "Daggonit, I told ya not to bother me. Lady's got some notion in her noggin that the calf is hers. I guess since it's black and white, it reminds her of Star. And her milk ain't dried up yet, so she's just gone a little crazy. She keeps lickin' the calf and tryin' to keep the cow away. And the cow ain't too happy, either."

And it was true—every time the poor cow took a step toward her calf, Lady pinned her ears, stomped her foot, and bared her teeth until the cow backed away in bewilderment. Then Lady turned and tenderly licked the top of the calf's head, nudging it gently toward her udder as if to help it nurse. The calf stood between the two, bawling in confusion.

"Oh, poor Lady!" Jody cried. "She misses Star so much! She's having a harder time than he is!"

"Well, I can't help that," Willie replied matter-of-factly. "That calf's got to nurse, and it ain't gonna be on Lady. Here, Jody, put this lead rope on her. She might not put up a fuss if you lead her away. I'll take care of the calf."

Jody fastened the lead to Lady's halter and turn

Every time the poor cow took a step toward her calf,
Lady pinned her ears and stomped her feet.

her head toward the willow tree while Mary patted her on the rump for encouragement. "C'mon, Lad, let's go see Gypsy. She misses you!" Mary prodded.

But Lady would have none of the idea of leaving her newly adopted calf. She planted her feet and would not move, and when Willie leaned down and wrapped his arms around the calf, picking it up in one quick motion to carry it to its mother, Lady reacted with a loud, high-pitched whinny. An instant later, a distraught whinny came in reply from the other side of the barn.

"Oh, no!" the girls groaned in unison. But the whinny from Star had the desired effect of making Lady forget her new baby and remember her old one, and she almost pulled the lead rope from Jody's hand in her haste to get to the gate and whinny back.

"Boy, she sure is fickle!" Mary laughed.

"She's what?" Jody replied crankily as Lady dragged her toward the gate.

"That means, 'not firm or steadfast.' That word was on my vocabulary test last week!"

At the gate, Jody unhooked the lead rope. Lady broke away, trotting up and down the fence line and whinny-ing in distress as the girls watched helplessly. Willie appeared just as she cantered back to the gate, stopped in her tracks, and with head up and ears forward, gazed longingly in the direction of Star's paddock.

"I got the cow and calf in the barnyard, and he's nursin' right good," he said casually. "Too bad Lady's takin' all this so hard."

"Willie, look, I think she's actually crying!" Jody said, pointing at the wet marks that had suddenly appeared in streaks from Lady's eyes almost to her muzzle. "Can animals cry?"

Willie took off his hat and scratched the side of his head. "Well, truth be told, it ain't the first time I seen an animal weep. They have emotions, just like us. They just don't show'em as much until somethin' really upsets 'em," he said, looking down at the two girls, who had tears running down their own cheeks. "Now, then, come on. She'll be all right in a few days. You just watch, when her milk dries up and you put Star back out here with her, she'll ignore him like she never saw him before. And look out if he tries to nurse on her—she'll whack him good!" he chuckled. "Now, get back over there and check on him. He's prob'ly not feelin' too good hisself."

"And he's with the rat!" Mary suddenly remembered, and the girls took off at a dead run, leaving Willie in the pasture shaking his head.

Star and the Squabs

MARY AND JODY decided after that first sleepless night that Star would be all right without them in the dark. And after all, as Willie said, he would have to learn to be by himself sometime. So after solemnly burying the rat and checking to make sure that Colonel Sanders was on his perch keeping Star company, they left him in his stall one more night. After that, they turned him out in the paddock overnight as they had always done when he was with Lady. As the days sped by, mother and son stopped calling to each other, and Star developed a voracious appetite for his hay and grain. By the end of the week, the girls got so bored just watching Star eat that they decided to take him for a walk like old times.

"Where should we go first, Mare?" Jody asked as she combed Star's half-black, half-white mane. "We could take him down by the creek and see if he wants to splash around in it."

"No, no, that means we would have to walk by the pasture and he would see Lady. I don't think he's ready for that yet. I'm a little worried about taking him out at all in case he tries to take off and run over to her."

"Oh, he's not going to do that. Are you, Star?" Jody asked, as Star rubbed his head up and down, up and down on her arm. "I honestly think he's forgotten all about Lady. And Willie said Lady's milk is almost dried up, so maybe we can turn them out together pretty soon."

"I know!" Mary said, jumping from her bale of hay and clapping her hands. "I almost forgot! Remember that day we helped Mr. McMurray load the straw wagon, and for payment he said we could get one of the squabs out of the pigeon house and adopt him and keep him for a pet? We could walk Star up to the pigeon house and pick out a squab! That's the opposite direction of the pasture!"

"I didn't know he said that! But let's do it! I can't wait! But . . . what is a squab, anyway?" Jody asked sheepishly.

"I didn't know either, at first," laughed Mary. "But I looked it up. It means, 'a nestling pigeon,' or a baby, in other words."

"Oh! OK, Star, you can help us pick one out. I think we should put your saddle on so you can get used to it on our trip around the farm," Jody said, giving Star an extra brushing on his back where the saddle would sit.

"Grand idea!" said Mary, already on her way to Jody's tack trunk to get out the saddle and girth. "He's already gotten used to it in the paddock, so he shouldn't mind it on a little walk."

The saddle was put on and the girth tightened, and the trio started out from Lucky Foot Stable on a walk up the gravel path toward Mr. McMurray's big stone house. The white pigeon house with the green-shingled roof sat in the farmyard next to the chicken house where Mary and Jody occasionally helped Mrs. McMurray gather the brown eggs from her Rhode Island Red hens. As they approached the farmyard,

Star pricked up his ears and raised his muzzle to the air, sniffing curiously at the unfamiliar smells drifting from the houses.

"Star, we brought you here once before, when you were little. Remember?" Jody whispered in his ear as she walked him straight to the pigeon house door. "But look, Mr. McMurray has the screen door on this time to keep it cool in there."

Wide-eyed, Star peered through the gray screen of the door and snorted inquisitively. At the strange noise, the startled pigeons flew from their perches with a whirring of wings and darted from wall to wall of the pigeon house in a frenzy. In response, Star snorted again and reared straight up in the air, almost knocking Jody off her feet!

"Jode! Hold on, I've got him!" Mary said, grabbing the lead rope tightly as Star came down, in anticipation of him trying to run off as fast as he could. But, to the girl's surprise, Star stood fast and stared inquisitively once more through the dusty screen.

"I don't think he's as scared as we thought," Jody said. "He just got startled for a second. Look, I think he wants to go in!"

And he did. Star extended his muzzle and pushed gingerly on the screen door, even taking a step forward as if to walk straight in if someone would only open the door wide enough.

"Do you think we should bring him in with us?" Jody wondered. "It would be good to get him used to scary things, and he definitely wants to see what's in there!"

"I don't see why not! I don't *think* Mr. McMurray would mind," Mary said hesitantly, looking around to make sure Mr. McMurray wasn't anywhere nearby.

"You open the door, and I'll lead him in," Jody instructed. "If we do it like Willie taught us when we were learning to load Lady onto the truck, like nothing out of the ordinary is happening, he should come right in!"

"Here goes!" Mary obliged.

Squueeeaaakkk, complained the rickety old door as Mary pushed it open. Star threw his head up in alarm, but he stood his ground and immediately stuck his head through the open door, sniffing nosily and taking another curious step forward.

"Come on, buddy," Jody encouraged. "Those old pigeons won't hurt you; they just fly around a lot and make all kinds of noise."

Jody pulled gently on Star's lead, and he pulled gently back, not quite sure about going all the way into the musty, dim pigeon house.

"Come on, Star," Mary said impatiently, "you have to help us pick out a squab to raise in Lucky Foot Stable. We don't have all day!"

"Give him time, Mare. It is pretty scary in there."

But Star didn't need any more time. His natural curiosity overcame him and he stepped boldly through the door, walking squarely to the center of the house and looking up wide-eyed at the pigeons, who were standing on their perches and gazing just as inquiringly back at him.

"Look, Mare, they're not even flying around! I thought they'd be in a panic when Star came in. I know they've never seen anything like him before!"

"Oh, yes, they have. These are homing pigeons, and Mr. McMurray lets them out once in a while to fly outside. They've seen cows and horses before. I bet they're more scared of us than they are of him! Come on, let's pick out a squab!"

Just then, a beautiful snow white bird with a shapely head and feathers all the way down his legs and feet sailed across the pigeon house, landing on a perch on the other side, and peered unruffled and dignified at the spectacle of two girls and a colt intruding upon his domain.

"Look, Jode! There's Sky King!" Mary exclaimed.

Mary had given this name to the stately pigeon one day after watching him glide through the air from perch to perch without having to flap his wings even once.

"He is gorgeous," Jody murmured. "Maybe we can find one of his babies that's as pretty as he is!"

Mary tiptoed quietly across the straw-covered floor of the pigeon house to the rows of nest boxes lining the far wall, Jody and Star following silently behind. The comforting *coo-r, coo-r* sound of contented pigeons filled the air, and all was peaceful in the house as Mary and Jody stood on tiptoe to look in the first box, where two tiny eggs lay unattended.

"I wonder why the mother isn't sitting on these and keeping them warm?" Jody asked.

"She probably flew off the nest when Star snorted. We better leave them alone, so she'll come back," Mary said knowledgeably.

The next nest in line was hung higher on the wall, prompting Mary to grab a bucket and turn it upside down on the floor as a step stool.

"Here, Jode, I'll steady the bucket while you stand on it and look in," Mary offered generously. "Look, Star is coming right along with you! He's not scared at all!"

Jody held Star's lead rope in her left hand as she

Star fell back on his haunches in astonishment, sending the pigeons flying madly once more.

stepped carefully on the upside-down bucket. With her right hand, she clutched the front of the nest and looked over the edge.

Whoooosh!! A mother pigeon burst from the nest directly into Jody's surprised face, knocking her from the bucket and onto her back in the middle of the straw and pigeon droppings, while Star fell back on his haunches in astonishment, sending the pigeons flying madly once more in a frenzy of whirring wings.

"Jody! Are you OK?" Mary yelled, trying to grab Jody's hand and Star's lead rope at the same time. Star righted himself, snorting and pawing and lowering his head to avoid the darting pigeons, while Mary attempted to help Jody up from the sticky straw. But Jody's feet slipped out from under her and down she went again, covering her britches with a second coating of pigeon mess. Star sniffed the sticky mass of pigeon droppings on the back of Jody's head, raised his nose, and lifted his top lip as horses do when they smell something funny. Jody put her hand in the goo and grimaced. This was too much for Mary. She lost her grip on Jody's other hand as she tried to suppress the belly laugh that rose from deep inside, worked its way up, and burst from her lips.

"Thanks, Mare. Thanks a lot," Jody scolded, but she couldn't help but laugh herself as Star lipped a strand of her hair and pushed her with his head as if to say, "Get up and get back to business!"

Jody pulled herself up from the gooey straw and set the overturned bucket back up as Mary took ahold of Star's rope.

"Alright, I'm going to look in that nest one more time, now that I know the mother is gone," Jody declared, bravely stepping onto the bucket once again and peering into the nest.

"What's in there?" Mary asked immediately. "How many eggs?"

"Oh, Mary, there are no eggs at all," Jody whispered.

"Well, go on to the next nest then," Mary instructed impatiently.

"No, no . . . there aren't any eggs, but there are two squabs! And they've got most of their feathers!"

"Let me see! Wait, I'll get another bucket!" Mary exclaimed, dragging Star with her. Soon she was standing next to Jody, gazing into the nest at the two spindly, knobby-beaked squabs while Star rubbed his head up and down on the side of her leg.

"Star, quit it! Oh, Jode, look at that white one! He must be Sky King's baby; but he's got black spots on his head and chest. I've never seen one like that before!"

"Look at the other one, poor thing," Jody murmured, touching the white squab's nestmate gently on top of its head. This squab was as plain as the other was beautiful—a dull gray with no special features—just like the pigeons that could be seen perched on statues in the city.

Jody reached in and cupped her hands gently under the soft white breast of the beautiful black-spotted squab, nestling it against her cheek to calm its struggling at her touch.

"Mary, he's perfect! Let's take him down to Lucky Foot and keep him as a pet until he can fly, and then we can set him free!"

Jody looked at Mary expectantly, waiting for her enthusiastic reply. But Mary wasn't looking at Jody or the pretty white squab. Her gaze was fixed on the forlorn, drab gray squab sitting quietly in the nest.

"Mary? Mare, what is it?" she asked.

Mary didn't answer, but she reached slowly into the nest, gently picking up the gray squab and cradling it in her hands.

"Jody," she said solemnly, "of course we want the beautiful squab. He's much prettier and nicer to look at, with his white feathers and rare black spots. But . . ."

Jody looked at Mary wide-eyed. "But what?"

"Well," Mary answered quietly, "why do we always pick the prettiest things? It's just not fair to the ones that aren't so pretty. If we leave the poor little gray guy here, he'll go to market and no one will ever care because he's not so pretty. They'll figure he wasn't good for anything but dinner anyway. I think we should choose him! He needs us! And look, he's already used to me!"

And he was. The dull little squab had nestled down in Mary's hand without a struggle, as if happy to be there. Even Star seemed to agree, sniffing the squab gently nose to beak as Mary held him out for the colt's approval. Jody sighed and set the white squab back in the nest.

"I guess you're right, Mare. He'll be happy in the stable with us. Let's go introduce him to Colonel Sanders—how do you think he'll feel about him?"

"Well, there's only one way to find out! Colonel Sanders, here we come!"

Colonel Saves the Day

COLONEL SANDERS HAPPENED to be in Lucky Foot Stable when Jody came in with Star in tow and Mary close behind, carrying their new friend. Cocking his head to the side and peering down from his perch on the top board of Lady's stall, he eyed the new addition with a mixture of curiosity and suspicion.

"Look, Colonel," called Mary, "it's . . . it's . . . well, who is it? We have to think of a name for him! Hmmm . . . let me see . . ."

"Mary?" Jody said timidly. "How about . . . well, what about . . ."

"Spit it out, Jody. What about what?"

"Well, do you remember that old movie we watched with your mom last week? Remember how we laughed when we saw the name of that one actor?"

"I remember laughing, but I don't remember the name of the actor."

"It was Walter, remember? Walter Pidgeon! Let's name him Walter!"

Mary looked solemnly at Jody, and then she began to laugh.

"Walter! Walter Pigeon!" she chuckled. "That's perfect! Walter it is! Now we have to make a home for him!"

Jody, suddenly feeling very proud of her suggestion, quickly made another one.

"How about the old bunny cage? We could fix it up just right for a bird."

"Excellent idea!" Mary agreed. "And after he gets used to it, we'll let him fly around the stable and teach him to go back to his cage to eat. Birds are very smart, you know."

Star used that moment to stretch out his muzzle to Walter once again, startling him so that one wing escaped Mary's grasp and smacked him soundly in

COLONEL SAVES THE DAY

the center of his nose. The girls laughed at Star's surprised expression as he snorted and shook his head.

Not to be outdone, Colonel Sanders suddenly let his presence be known by standing to his full height, flapping his wings, and letting out a very indignant, "Ba-bawk!"

"Oh, Colonel, calm down," Mary scolded. "You'll see, Walter will keep you company."

"You can help him get settled in," added Jody generously.

"All right, troops, enough introductions for one day. Walter's tired," observed Mary, dragging the old bunny cage away from the wall where it had stood unoccupied for the past year. "Jody, put Star in his stall. It's time to get Walter's house ready."

The girls could not bring themselves to mention the previous occupant of the cage, a brown-and-white lop-eared bunny named Uncle Wiggly, who had come to a sad demise the previous summer. The day had been too hot to ride, and Mary and Jody had decided to give the stable a thorough cleaning. Together they had picked up the rabbit cage with Uncle Wiggly inside and set it outside the stable door in the paddock, intending to keep it there just long enough to rake and sweep the dirt floor where it stood. Well, the truth was that they had gotten so involved in cleaning and raking and talking and giggling that they forgot poor old Uncle Wiggly. By the time they remembered the unfortunate bunny, he had passed out from the heat, and no matter how hard they fanned him and begged him to revive, he lay still as death. Mary even tried rubbing him down with cold water—a trick she had learned in a book once—but to no avail. Poor Uncle Wiggly never woke up. The girls had conducted a very solemn ceremony for him, burying him by the corncrib and erecting a cross made of willow switches in his honor.

Mary dragged the cage to the middle of the stable, and the girls surveyed it in silence.

"Poor old Uncle Wiggly," Jody finally whispered.

"May he rest in peace, and we'll say no more," Mary answered solemnly. Then, after a deep sigh, she continued briskly, "Well, time's a-wastin.' We can't cry over spilled milk. The cage will be put to good use now. Uncle Wiggly would be glad."

"Mary, isn't it a good thing the cage has such a high roof? It'll be just perfect for a bird," observed Jody.

"Yep, and you know, we'll let him out a lot too. He won't be caged up all the time."

"He'll need a food bowl, a water bowl, and a bath-tub," Jody decided. "Birds like to take baths, you know."

"And he needs grit. All birds have to have grit for their gizzards, so they can digest their food," Mary added knowingly. "I read that in a book once. And as for watering, watch this!"

Mary walked over to the stable water pump, pulled up the handle, cupped her hands under the flowing water, and took some in her mouth. Then she took Walter from Jody's grasp, opened her mouth so that her tongue was rolled back and her jaw made sort of a water bowl, and pushed Walter's head gently down so that his beak just touched the water.

"Mary!" shrieked Jody. "What are you doing?!"

At the shocked expression on Jody's face, Mary laughed so hard she spit the water across the stable. "I'm teaching him how to drink from my mouth! It's an ancient Indian custom. I think. I don't know, I read about it somewhere. Watch. I'll try again. I think he's going to get it!"

So Mary again took in some water and gently pushed Walter's beak into her open mouth. To Jody's amazement, the plucky bird sipped some of the water and tilted his head back to swallow it, as birds do.

"Mary, did you see that? He drank some!" Jody yelped.

Mary could only nod slightly as she held Walter close to her open mouth. This time he cocked his head to one side, eyed the welcoming water, and took a drink with no encouragement. Jody giggled with delight as Colonel Sanders clucked indignantly and shook his head at the scandalous behavior. Mary spit out the rest of the water and held Walter up, looking him directly in the eye.

"Walter," she said solemnly, "you are going to be all right. After your feathers grow and you can fly, we'll let you out so you can have your freedom. But never forget, we are now eternally bonded." Walter only blinked. "Now, let's get your cage ready!"

While the girls busied themselves scrubbing water and feed bowls and preparing a comfortable home for Walter, an unwelcome guest crept into the stable and silently leapt onto an old shelf and then up to the wooden rafters above their heads. Creeping slowly, his belly low on the rough boards, the creature surveyed the activity below with his round yellow eyes. His name was Beamer, but his reputation for catching mice on the farm had prompted Mary to give him the title Supreme Barn Mouser. Unseen by the girls, he sat directly above them and began nonchalantly cleaning his black and white fur as they ruffled the bed of straw in the corner of the old bunny cage, arranging it just so. Meanwhile, Walter sat motionless where the girls had placed him in a small cardboard box on a stool in front of Star's stall, awaiting his new home.

"He won't fly out." Mary had declared as they placed him in the box. "His wings aren't ready yet."

Beamer rested on the rafter like a lion on a tree limb, blinking lazily as he watched the girls. He had almost lost interest and was turning to go in search of mice when the sound of Walter's claws scratching the bottom of the box caught his attention. Beamer's eyes widened and his ears pricked up as he crouched again, his head shaking slightly with excitement as he eyed the unsuspecting squab scrabbling and pecking at the bottom of the box. Mary and Jody didn't notice as Beamer crept ever so slowly to the end of the beam until he was directly above Walter.

"OK, Jody, get the bowls. The cage is almost ready," Mary said, oblivious to the menace overhead. Jody went out to the paddock to retrieve the small white crockery bowls from the spot in the sun where

Then he swooped down upon the escaping cat with every talon bared!

the girls had placed them to dry. Meanwhile, Beamer gazed down, measuring the distance he would have to jump from the rafters to the top board of Star's stall. Finally, he gathered himself and leapt, landing nimbly on the board and teetering for just an instant before regaining his balance. Star started at the sight of the cat, but he soon lost interest and went back to munching his hay. Poor Walter, on the other hand, became so frightened upon seeing the cat not two feet above his head that he scrabbled frantically in his box and flapped his wings in terror.

"All right, all right, Walter! Your home is almost ready. Calm down!" Mary yelled, not turning from the cage to see what the matter was. Then, in the blink of an eye, Beamer was in and out of the box and running across the stable with Walter in his jaws!

"Beamer!" screamed Mary as the murderous cat flew past her toward the small crack between the stable doors where he had crept in earlier.

"Walter!" Jody screeched, running in from the paddock and racing with Mary to attempt a rescue. Beamer had not anticipated the size of Walter, who was much bigger than a mouse, and he was finding it impossible to get himself and the pigeon through the crack all at once. With the girls almost upon him,

Beamer turned and raced back to the front of the stable where he could make his escape by jumping
through the low window there. But just as he
crouched to make the leap, Colonel Sanders, from
the top board of Lady's stall, drew himself up to his
full height, squawked, and flapped his wings menac-
ingly. Then he swooped down upon the escaping cat
with every talon bared! Beamer yowled in pain as the
Colonel's claws found his flesh, and Walter dropped
at last from the astonished cat's open jaws. Beamer
escaped the clutches of the Colonel long enough to
make it through the window, but the Colonel continued after him, flapping and squawking in full pursuit.

"Oh, Walter!" Mary cried, kneeling by the squab
where he lay on his side on the dirt floor.

"Mary, is he dead?" Jody asked fearfully, her voice
quivering.

Mary picked Walter up gently, and as she did, he
opened his eyes and blinked.

"Phew! I thought so for a second. He's so petrified
his heart is beating a mile a minute! And," she said,
examining the skin under his feathers, "he's got a
little blood on him where Beamer's old teeth went
into his skin."

"Not a very nice first day!" Jody exclaimed, stroking Walter's head sympathetically. "We'll have to clean him up a little."

"Did you see the Colonel?" Mary asked with a chuckle.

"I couldn't believe it!" Jody exclaimed. "Did you ever expect him to do something like that? He's really earned the name Colonel now!"

"I have a feeling the old Colonel's been waiting for years to get that old cat for something, and this just gave him a good excuse! Now, we'd better get Walter cleaned up and in his cage, and we have to make sure the top is secure!"

So Walter was placed lovingly in his bed of straw with full bowls of food and water, and as the girls watched quietly, he settled into a corner, ruffled his fuzzy breast, tucked his tired head behind his wing, and fell fast asleep.

Circus Act

IN THE SPAN of just a few weeks, Walter' wings had developed so that he could fly effortlessly around Lucky Foot Stable. His favorite resting spot was on the top board of Lady's stall, close to the Colonel. It was almost as if he knew the old white rooster had saved his life, and he seemed content and happy to be one of the family. Now when Mary and Jody rode their bikes to the stable at the crack of dawn on weekend mornings, the first thing they did was to free Walter from his cage.

On one such warm and sunny morning, the girls met in the stable early as usual. After feeding and grooming Star and releasing Walter—who immediately flew to his roosting spot and began preening his feathers—they went to sit under the weeping willow tree in the middle of the big pasture and talk about their plans for the day.

"Mare, it's such a nice morning, and you know we haven't ridden since Lady and Star were separated," Jody hinted as they watched Lady and Gypsy graze peacefully with the cows.

"I know, it seemed like she was too upset before, and we didn't want her to see Star. What do you think she would do if she saw him now?"

"I don't know, Mare, I still don't think they should see each other, at least not until Willie says it's OK. So we can't ride past Lucky Foot, and the only way to ride off the farm is past Lucky Foot," Jody moaned.

"That means we can't go to Secret Place, or the Piney Wood, or even the field where the Christmas trees are."

The girls sat in perplexed silence, watching the ponies swat flies with their tails.

"Mary, I have an idea!" Jody suddenly said. "Why don't we practice our circus act right here in the pasture? The cows could be our audience!"

"Not bad, not bad," Mary said thoughtfully. "Let's ask the ponies what they think. Gypsy! Ladabucks!

Do you want to practice our circus act today?"

The girls laughed when Lady snorted loudly and Gypsy shook her head, just as though they had understood the question.

"Lady thinks the cows are too stupid to appreciate our death-defying trick riding!" Mary chuckled.

"And Gypsy is just lazy!" Jody added. "But I think it's a good idea. Cows are a better audience than nothing, I guess. And we do need the practice."

Mary and Jody weren't practicing for a real circus, of course. But they had come up with a real circus act anyway, and it had been a long time since they had worked on it.

"Let's run to the stable and get our helmets and the bridles. And we can say hello to Star and make sure Walter isn't getting attacked again," Mary said, jumping up from the grass. "Be right back, Lad and Gypsy!"

The girls were back in the pasture with the necessary equipment almost before the ponies knew they were gone. Bridles and helmets were put on in a jiffy, and the girls mounted up bareback. It was time for the circus act to begin!

As Mary and Jody cantered around the pasture to warm up, the cows continued to graze peacefully, unaware of the exciting events about to transpire. Of course, Mary decided it was her job to get their attention. She reined Gypsy to a halt in the center of the pasture and stood on the cooperative pony's back, her sneakered feet planted firmly on the generous flesh on either side of the mare's backbone. Jody giggled as she watched from a seated position on Lady.

Holding the bridle reins in one hand and gesturing grandly with the other, Mary addressed her audience.

"Ladies and gentlemen!" Mary hollered in her best ringmaster voice, "today we will present to you our act, a circus act, an act of death-defying courage and riding trickery such as the world has never seen! Was that bad grammar?" Mary asked Jody. Jody nodded and giggled some more. A few cows raised their heads.

"Anyway, ladies and germs, we shall begin today by introducing our fearless, beautiful, and well-trained steeds—the indescribable flaxen chestnut mare from the highlands of Europe, Gypsy Amber . . ." (Jody applauded enthusiastically.) "And accompanying her in the fantastic and incredible spectacle you are about to witness, straight from the wild and untamed Western plains, raised and trained by the Indians, the painted mare, Lady White Cloud!"

At this, Jody raised herself to stand on Lady's back and bow grandly to the audience. Several more cows looked up at the curious sight of the girls standing side by side on the ponies, but they soon lost interest and dropped their heads again to graze.

"Now, let's start the show!" bellowed Mary.

On cue, the girls clasped each other's hands in the air, dropped their reins, and raised their free hands in a majestic salute to the audience. At the same moment, their feet slid down the ponies' sides and they were seated on the pony's backs for just an instant before sliding back with their hands still clasped, off the hind ends of the ponies, landing on their feet in the pasture. The well trained and amazing Gypsy and Lady stood perfectly still while Mary and Jody, in unison, took three giant steps backwards, then ran and vaulted onto the pony's backs again from behind.

"A trick we learned from watching the unforgettable Western movie actor, Mr. John Wayne!" Mary announced proudly. Again in unison, the girls gently slapped the shoulders of their mounts with their right hands and then raised them to the sky in another grand gesture of the circus.

"For our next feat, we will demonstrate the astounding agility and dexterity of these fearless beasts as we guide them through the serpentine!

*The girls clasped each other's hands in the air, dropped
their reins, and raised their hands in a salute.*

Note the flying lead changes executed by Lady White Cloud and Gypsy Amber as they maneuver around each pole!"

The serpentine was a straight line of rickety fence posts at the side of the pasture that had not been removed when the new fence was put up. The ten posts were just the right distance apart for a pony to snake through, in and out all the way down the line.

"The challenge, ladies and gems, is to ride this difficult course at a canter—that is, faster than a trot and slower than a gallop—without the rider's legs touching the posts, or banging into them, which is a most painful occurrence, as we well know from our years of practice!"

The girls trotted Lady and Gypsy to opposite ends of the serpentine and then turned to face each other. The ponies pranced with excitement, remembering this trick from previous rehearsals.

"Aaaaannnddd . . . on your marks, get set, GO!" screamed Mary. Jody leaned forward and Lady took off at a canter, swerving through the posts at a fearful rate but with such skill that Jody's legs never brushed any of the posts. At the end of the line, Jody slapped Mary's outstretched hand, and Mary took off in the opposite direction on Gypsy, whooping and hollering through the posts with one hand in the air.

After the last post, Mary reined Gypsy in and trotted calmly to Lady and Jody. The girls again saluted the crowd, none of whom were paying the slightest bit of attention.

"And now, ladies and gents, for our final and most awe-inspiring performance of all, we will attempt—and I did say attempt—a stunt that has not been performed since Buffalo Bill's Wild West Show, by none other than the world famous Miss Annie Oakley! Now, *riders dismount!*

The girls swung their legs over the ponies and landed at the same instant on the ground.

"But before we attempt this trick, we will demonstrate the quiet nature of our mounts once more, while at the same time rewarding them for a job well done so far today!"

At that, Mary crawled behind Gypsy's front legs and Jody behind Lady's, and sitting cross-legged, they each grasped a front leg of their pony in each hand, looking at their audience between the pony's legs as if behind bars. A sugar cube was produced from each girl's pocket and held just beyond each pony's reach as Mary continued:

"Now, Gypsy. Now, Lady. You may accept your rewards, and *take a bow!*"

The ponies dipped their heads to take the sugar cubes held in the girls' outstretched palms, giving the illusion of a bow to the audience.

"Thank you, thank you!" Jody and Mary exclaimed grandly to the imaginary applause.

"Enough of this nonsense, now for the grand finale!" Mary shouted as the girls crawled from under their ponies and faced the audience. "Watch carefully now, as we vault onto our fearless steed's backs at the trot, and without missing a beat, retrieve a minuscule scrap of cloth otherwise known as a handkerchief from the ground while hanging precariously by one leg! And all with no visible means of support! Jody, the handkerchief, please!"

"The handkerchief?" Jody asked blankly.

"Yes, the handkerchief!" Mary repeated loudly. Jody searched her pockets frantically.

"The one around your neck," Mary finally whispered from the corner of her mouth.

"Oh! Sorry," Jody said sheepishly, untying and whisking the red bandana dramatically from her neck and handing it to Mary with a flourish.

"Now, we will drop the handkerchief halfway

down the field while avoiding the cow pies, and after a running vault which will amaze and astound you, we will canter down and retrieve it from the ground using methods previously described!"

Jody's heart began beating a little faster in anticipation of this, the most difficult trick in their circus repertoire. The last time they had attempted the trick, the pickup item had been a very large burlap bag, not a very small handkerchief. But Mary didn't seem the least bit worried as she dropped the handkerchief in the middle of the cow pasture and trotted back to where Jody stood with Lady. As Mary dismounted from Gypsy, Jody made her first announcement of the day.

"Ladies and gentlemen, Mary and Gypsy will be first!" she declared grandly.

"Oh, we will, will we?" Mary laughed. "Alrighty, then, my partner has nominated me to be the first to attempt this death-defying demonstration of riding skill not seen since the days of the Wild West! Oh, and one more thing—do not attempt this at home!"

Mary slapped Gypsy lightly on the hindquarters, urging her into a slow trot. Trotting along beside her, Mary grasped her mane and vaulted onto Gypsy's back just as she began to canter.

"Mary, be careful!" Jody yelled as Mary approached the handkerchief at a brisk canter. Her breath caught in her throat as Mary grasped Gypsy's mane firmly in her left hand and slid off to the side, as the lower half of her left leg hooked over the mare's back and her free hand reached for the small scrap of red cloth.

"Yeeehaaa!" Mary screeched as she grabbed the handkerchief and twirled it in a circle above her head while Gypsy cantered on. Then, "aaaaaghhh!" she continued, trying to right herself on Gypsy's back but instead tumbling off into the cow pasture in a heap. The minute Gypsy felt herself with no rider, she stopped in her tracks and turned to look at Mary as if to say, "Whatever happened to you?"

"Mary! Are you OK?" Jody asked breathlessly, reaching her friend seconds later.

"Of course I'm OK!" Mary declared. "And if I hadn't landed smack dab in the middle of this fresh cow pie, I'd be perfect!" she continued, holding out her right hand, which was completely covered in greenish muck. "Can you help me up?"

"Help you up? Not with that hand, I can't." Jody laughed. "Eeewww!"

"Well here, then, this one's clean," she said,

offering her left hand for Jody to pull her to her feet.

"Eeewww, Mare, look at your britches! And *your hair!*"

Without thinking, and being right handed, Mary reached around with her muck-covered hand and felt the back of her muck-covered hair, and continued down to touch the back of her muck-covered britches. Jody burst out laughing uncontrollably as Gypsy extended her muzzle and sniffed the offending area and snorted loudly, curling her upper lip to the sky as horses do when they smell something particularly unpleasant. Mary, undaunted and mindful of her showmanship, simply turned to her audience with a flourish.

"Ladies and gents, as you well know, even with the best and most accomplished of trick riders, mishaps do occasionally occur—at times due to the unpredictable nature of the mount and at other times due to the clumsiness of the rider. What you have witnessed today was an unsurpassed demonstration of the clumsiness of the rider!"

Jody continued to laugh and the cows continued to graze.

"Anyway, and with no further ado, we thank you for your patience today and we hope you have enjoyed at least most of our show. We look forward to seeing you at our next event, and please, watch your step as you exit."

Mary turned from her audience, and the girls unbridled the ponies and watched as Gypsy and Lady trotted off across the pasture. Then they turned and walked to the pasture gate with Jody still giggling and Mary's head held high with as much dignity as she could muster, all the while limping slightly as she favored the wet side of her britches.

The first thing Mary did when the girls got back to Lucky Foot Stable was to raise the handle on the red water pump, wash off her hands, and bend over, flinging her hair upside down under the running water. Star nickered curiously from his stall at the sight, and Colonel Sanders and Walter cocked their heads inquisitively from their perch on the top board.

"Can't do much about the britches right now," Mary murmured to herself as she craned her neck, hair dripping, to try and assess the damage behind. Walter chose just that moment to glide from his perch and land squarely on Mary's head, pecking at a wet strand of her hair.

Jody, about to hang her bridle on its rack, turned

just in time to witness the spectacle of Mary curled around for a view of her stained britches, trying to remain motionless so as not to disturb Walter, who busily squeezed a drink of water from her hair with his beak.

"Joodde . . ." Mary giggled low in her throat to keep from jiggling Walter, but Jody couldn't help it . . . she laughed so hard she dropped her bridle and fell to her knees on the dirt floor of Lucky Foot Stable.

★ 9 ★

The Reunion

THE NEXT DAY dawned warm and bright, and Mary and Jody had just arrived at Lucky Foot Stable when Willie appeared in the doorway, scratching his head and pulling on his earlobe the way he always did when he was about to make a pronouncement.

"Willie!" Mary said excitedly. "You missed our circus act! We practiced yesterday in the pasture field . . ."

"And then Mary landed in a cow plop, and Walter landed on her head when she washed her hair, and . . ."

"Walter who?" Willie asked, peering into the old bunny cage. "Oh, you mean that ugly little squab? He looks like he's about ready for the stewpot."

"Willie!" exclaimed Jody. "He's not ugly! Well, maybe a little. And he's not a squab anymore, he's a full-grown pigeon now. Watch, we'll let him out of his cage. He doesn't even try to fly away. He stays right here with us."

"I don't have time for this foolishness," Willie interrupted, looking out the stable door into the paddock. "I came over here to see if you're ready to put this ornery bugger and his mama back together again."

"Ornery bugger . . . you mean Star? Do you think this is a good time? Is he ready? Is Lady's milked dried up yet?" Mary asked breathlessly.

"Slow down, girl. Yes, Lady's milk is dried up and he's as ready as he's ever gonna git. Now here's a lead rope . . . grab ahold of Star and we'll lead him over to the pasture. I let the cows into the barn a little early, so's he wouldn't have to git used to them at first."

"That's right! He's never really seen a cow up close. I wonder if he'll be scared?" Jody asked.

"That's what I mean. I figure we'll let him out in the pasture with Lady and Gypsy, and then later on when the cows come back out, he'll at least be settled down a little already."

"Good plan, Willie," Mary said approvingly as Jody snapped the lead rope onto Star's halter and led him from the paddock. "I can't wait to see what Star does when he sees Lady!"

Willie just shook his head as the three approached the cow pasture with Star in tow. Nearing the gate, Star suddenly started prancing and throwing his head up and down.

"Whoa, buddy!" Jody exclaimed, trying to hold Star steady. But it was too late. Star had seen Lady over the pasture gate, and he reacted by letting out a long shrill whinny.

At the familiar sound, Lady and Gypsy raised their heads from grazing at the exact same moment, still chewing. Then they switched their tails lazily and resumed grazing.

"Look, Willie! Lady doesn't even act like she remembers him!" Jody exclaimed as Mary unhooked the chain on the gate.

"I been tellin' you that," Willie responded. "Just watch."

At that, Mary pushed open the gate and Jody unhooked the lead rope from Star's halter.

Before Jody could even pat him good-bye, Star took off at a canter across the pasture, heading straight for Lady and whinnying all the way.

"Willie, she'll be happy to see him, won't she?" Jody worried.

"Anything could happen," Willie replied mysteriously. "Just wait and see."

It didn't take long for Star to reach Lady, and when he did, he wasted no time trying to get reacquainted. Nickering happily, Star extended his muzzle to Lady's in typical horse greeting fashion. And Lady responded, ears up, sniffing Star's nostrils.

"Look, Willie. She *is* happy to see him!" Mary cried.

"So far," Willie replied quietly.

Before the words were barely out of Willie's mouth, Lady pinned her ears against her head, kicked out with one front hoof, and made a horrible grunting sound of intense displeasure in Star's direction. Star threw his head up in shock, his initial joy at seeing his mother turning suddenly to astonishment. Lady moved away a few steps and continued grazing with Gypsy.

"Willie, why did she do that?" Jody asked in dismay. "She's acting so mean!"

Willie didn't reply but continued to watch with a half-grin on his face. Star, having partially overcome his initial amazement at Lady's behavior, decided to try again. He gingerly took a step in Lady's direction and stood gazing at her, his ears up in question, as if to say, "Mama, don't tell me you don't remember me!" Taking a few more tentative steps, he stretched out his neck as far as it would go without having to step any closer, and pointed his muzzle toward her flank as if to nuzzle for milk.

This time Lady pinned her ears and lunged at him, teeth bared, then turned suddenly and kicked with both hind feet, barely missing Star's head.

"Lady!" screamed Mary and Jody in unison. Jody's hand was on the gate to go in and rescue Star when Willie grabbed her arm and actually laughed out loud.

"Willie! It's not funny! I have to go in and save him! Lady is trying to kill him!" she beseeched.

"She's not trying to kill him, no such a thing," Willie replied calmly. "She's just puttin' him in his place, is all. She's teachin' him that he's on his own now and should be startin' to act grown up, not like a baby wantin' to nurse. You just leave them be. They'll get on all right in a little while."

Mary and Jody watched in silence, and they had to admit to themselves that the expression on Star's

This time Lady pinned her ears and lunged at him,
teeth bared, then turned suddenly and kicked.

face was almost comical as he stood a safe distance from Lady, gazing at her with his head cocked to one side, both mortified and confused. Lady had gone back to grazing peacefully, thoroughly ignoring her son as if he were just another cow in the pasture.

This was too much for Star. Mary and Jody could almost see the thoughts turning in his brain as he decided he would get Lady's attention any way he could. Suddenly tossing his head and letting out an impudent squeal, he took off at a gallop across the pasture, bucking and kicking and spinning in circles like a rodeo horse. Skidding to a stop at the fence line, he turned and galloped back toward Lady, repeating his antics all the way. He halted squarely in front of her and snorted, nostrils flaring like a stallion, and reared to his full height. And then he dropped to the ground and rolled over and over.

"Willie, what in the world is he doing?" Mary giggled. "I just hope he's not rolling in any green cow plops; he'll really make a fool of himself then!"

"He's just showin' off—tryin' to make her look at him. But look, she don't care one way or th' other," he chuckled. And he was right. Lady simply went on grazing as if Star was nothing more than a pesky old fly. "I got to get back to the cow stable—the cows'll think I forgot to milk 'em." Willie continued. "You just stay out of that pasture and let them get together in their own good time."

Star finished rolling and lay still in the pasture, catching his breath and scrutinizing Lady's reaction to his mischief out of the corner of one eye. Seeing that she had no reaction at all, he sighed heavily and raised his head, blinking at her in frustration.

"Poor baby, look at him," Jody murmured. "He doesn't understand."

"I know. I didn't know Lady could be so mean," Mary added. "She's usually so sweet."

As if hearing Mary's comment, Lady raised her head from the grass and looked directly into Star's wide eyes. The two stood gazing at each other for a moment, and then Lady stepped quietly to her impish son. Star rolled his eyes and looked ready to flee, but he remained lying down as Lady sniffed his muzzle gently. Then she simply licked him once on the top of his head before turning back to her grazing. Star's eyes widened and he shook his head. Then, understanding that everything was all right at last, he raised himself from the ground and took his place in the pasture next to Lady, grazing as calmly as if he had never left her side.

10

Swinging

"MARE, MAYBE WE should come back out here when the cows are turned out after milking, so we can see how Star reacts," Jody declared as the girls walked back to Lucky Foot Stable from the pasture field, satisfied that Star and Lady were getting on all right, as Willie had predicted.

"I know," Mary agreed. "But what should we do in the meantime?"

"Well, we could go climb the horse chestnut tree and shell some corn for the ducks," Jody suggested.

"We really should clean Star's stall, so when we

bring him back in it'll be ready," Mary said half-heartedly. "Or we could just leave him in the paddock tonight. It's not going to rain, and it's warm out," she continued.

"Do you think Mr. McMurray will ever let him stay out in the pasture with Lady and Gypsy all the time?" Jody wondered.

"Probably not," Mary replied glumly. "Remember what Willie said."

It had taken quite a bit of effort on Willie's part to talk Mr. McMurray into allowing even two ponies to graze in the pasture all day and night with his cows. "Hayburners!" he had called the ponies. "And eating up my profits, they are." Willie had explained to the girls that Mr. McMurray was being very generous as it was, and although Mr. McMurray had grudgingly agreed to allow them to turn Star out in the pasture for a short time each day, he would have to come in to either his stall or the paddock at night.

"I know what we can do!" Mary exclaimed. "Let's fix up our hay fort and swing on the rope swing in the barn! We haven't done that for ages!"

"Good plan!" agreed Jody. "Then we can listen for Willie to turn out the cows and go watch Star when he does!"

So the girls dashed to the top of the barn hill and took a firm hold on the immense sliding barn door that led to the enormous hayloft of Mr. McMurray's dairy cow barn.

"Ready, one, two, three!" they shouted in unison, and the door began to slide slowly open as they pushed with all their might. Pigeons flew overhead with a whirring of wings as the girls entered through the narrow opening their effort had afforded them. They stood quietly in the cavernous structure, which was lined on either side with neatly stacked mountains of hay and straw, and blinked as their eyes adjusted to the dim light.

"Gosh, Jode, I think the last time we were up here was when Willie showed us the sleigh!" Mary exclaimed.

"That reminds me—next winter when it snows, it'll be Lady's turn to learn how to pull it!"

Jody said excitedly. "Remember, she was so pregnant with Star at Christmas that Willie said she could learn next time!"

"Yeah, and we were so dumb we didn't even know why Lady was so fat!" Mary chuckled.

"Hey, let's go in the grain room and see how the old sleigh's doing!"

To the left of where the girls stood was a room built into the side of the barn, where wheat, barley, and oats were stored in individual bins, waiting to be ground into feed for the dairy cows.

Mary creaked open the rickety door and the girls went in slowly, peering around at the cobwebbed corners and taking in the smell of the variety of grains. In the furthest corner of the room, the canvas-covered form of the sleigh could be seen in the faint light. Mary and Jody tiptoed toward it, feeling the need to be quiet and still in the stuffy room. Just as they were passing the last bin of wheat on their right, a fat brown groundhog darted out of the barley bin on the left and stood up on his hind legs, chattering a warning to get out of his room!

"AAAGHHH!" Mary screamed, so startled by this sudden apparition that she turned and tripped over Jody, and they both fell in a heap on the dusty floor. Disturbed by Mary's scream, a suddenly awakened barn owl swooped down just inches from the girls' heads and flew out the door, its giant wing knocking over a grain shovel with a clatter on its way out. Mary and Jody screamed again and crawled on their hands and knees as fast as they could go until they reached the relative safety of the barn floor and sat shuddering, holding each other's hands.

"I don't think I want to see the sleigh that bad," Mary whispered, forgetting her good grammar for the moment. Then the girls looked at each other sheepishly and burst out laughing.

"You should have seen your face!" Jody giggled. "You looked like you saw a ghost!"

"I thought I did!" Mary laughed. "And you should talk—you were as white as a sheet!

But anyway, enough of this foolishness, time's a-wastin.' Willie will be done milking soon, and we haven't even started on our fort! But look, the swing is still there, same as always!"

The swing of which Mary spoke was simply a long braided rope with a large knot tied on the end, hanging straight down from the rafters of the barn. A tall pile of hundreds of bales of hay stacked neatly against the barn wall rose to one side of the rope, and a stack of the same height of straw towered on the other, but the stacks were much too far from the rope and the rope hung at least ten feet from the floor—too far for the girls to grab it without piling some bales underneath and standing on them to reach.

"Looks like we've got work to do," Mary exclaimed. "First we'll have to climb up to the top of the high stack and throw some bales down, and then we'll stack them under the rope so we can reach it. Let's use straw—it's not as heavy as hay."

So up the bales of straw they clambered like mountain climbers, until they reached the top layer, where they were able to push and throw enough bales to the floor to build a pile high enough to stand on and reach the rope. When they were finished, they stood back to admire their handiwork.

"That's a good sturdy stack, if I do say so myself," Mary bragged.

"Hey, what about me? I built it too, you know," Jody chided.

"Yes, you did, and now I think you should climb up there and see if you can grab the rope. You're a little taller than me," Mary proposed. "I'll climb up partway and hold on to your ankles."

"Me? I'm barely taller than you, and you're the one who's so fearless—remember climbing up the pine tree to cut the top out?"

"Yes, and that's why it's your turn now," Mary insisted. "Just go up there and grab the rope, and I'll hold your ankles while you try to throw the knotty end up onto the high stack. Then we'll be able to swing practically across the whole barn!"

Jody gave Mary one last desperate look, took a deep breath, and turned to the stack of bales. The bottom of the stack was wide and sturdy with ten bales in a square, but it narrowed as it went up until there were only two bales for Jody to stand on at the very top.

"Mare, it feels kind of shaky up here," Jody lamented as she stood with one foot on each of the bales.

"Never fear! I've got you," Mary crowed, sitting up on her knees on the third layer of bales and grabbing one of Jody's ankles in each hand. "Now just reach up and grab it!"

"But it's just about two inches too high!" Jody insisted, stretching up as tall as she could on her tip-toes to reach the elusive knot.

"All right then, you'll have to jump a little to grab it," Mary prodded.

"But I'm going to fall!" Jody cried, beginning to wish she hadn't ever suggested swinging to begin with.

"No, you're not. Just try it. Jump a little and see if you can get ahold of it."

So Jody jumped. But when she grabbed the knot,

the momentum swung her out and off the stack of bales and then back over the stack like a pendulum. Her feet were just about two inches too high to get back on the bale.

"Mare! What do I do?" Jody screeched, holding tight to the knotted rope as she swung back and forth.

"Wait—there, I've got you again," Mary soothed, grabbing Jody's ankles as she swung over. "Calm down, and just drop back down on the two top bales again! You're only a little bit above them!"

"But they're not very sturdy! What if I don't drop right and they topple over?"

"What in the world is goin' on in here?" A familiar voice came gruffly from the barn doorway.

"Willie!" Jody yelled, never so relieved to see the old cowhand. "Mary made me climb up here to get the rope, and now I've got it, and I can't let it go!"

"I didn't actually make her, Willie. It was just a suggestion," Mary squeaked.

Willie didn't say a word. He just shook his head as he hobbled over to the stack of bales. He climbed deftly up next to Mary and wrapped one arm around Jody's waist.

"Now let go and drop down a little. I got ya." Willie said grumpily.

Jody released the rope immediately, knowing she'd

better obey with no complaint. Her feet came down solidly on the bales, and she breathed a sigh of relief.

"Now, would you two mind tellin' me just what you're tryin' to do?" Willie demanded, stepping down to the barn floor and turning to Mary.

"Well, Willie, we just wanted to swing on the rope, and we couldn't reach it, so we had to stack up some bales, and Jody was going to grab the end and throw it up to the top of the big stack, so we could go up there and swing across the barn," Mary said all in one breath.

"And did ya think she was goin' to be able to throw the rope while she was swingin' on it just now?" Willie asked crankily.

"I guess we didn't really think that far ahead," Mary replied sheepishly.

"Good thing I came up here to throw some feed down the chute," Willie said. "Can you think of any more mischief to get into now, or can I get back to feedin'?"

"No, no, Willie, no more mischief at all," Jody said quickly.

As Willie turned toward the grain room, Mary said meekly, "Um, Willie?"

Willie turned back, his face like a thunderbolt.

"What now?" he growled.

Mary put on her sweetest voice. "Uh, while you're here, and since you're taller than us, do you think you could just take a second to climb back up on our stack and throw the rope up for us? Please?"

Willie took off his farm cap and scratched the side of his head. Then he looked up at the hayloft and back at the two pleading faces. "Daggone girls," he muttered, but hobbled over and climbed silently up the stack and onto the top two bales, taking hold of the knotty end of the rope and with one motion flinging it easily up to the top bales of the loft.

"Are ya happy?" he groused, heading back to the grain room to finish feeding the cows.

"Yes, Willie! Thanks ever so!" Mary cried. "C'mon, Jode, time's a'wastin'! Last one to the top of the hayloft is a rotten egg!"

Once at the top of the loft, the girls' brave resolve began to fade as they looked down at the barn floor twenty feet below them, but neither would admit it to the other.

"You go first, Mare," Jody said, patting Mary on the back encouragingly. "This looks really fun!"

"Me, go first? Why me? I went first the other day

in the circus act. And come to think of it, you never did go after me!"

"That's because I was too busy laughing at you landing in the cow plop. And I *was* the one who just climbed up to try and reach the rope!"

"Oh, this is ridiculous," Mary said, "what are we worried about? We used to swing on the rope all the time!"

"That's when we were young and not afraid of anything," Jody replied. Suddenly realizing the silliness of Jody's comment, the girls looked at each other and burst out laughing.

"All right, enough of this nonsense," Mary exclaimed. "I will go first in remembrance of days past when we were little and fearless." And without another word, she grabbed the rough rope just above the knot and pushed off.

"YEEEHHHAAAA!" Mary squealed as she sailed through the air and across the empty space of the barn to the opposite side, where she landed atop the high stack of straw.

"Mare! Are you OK?" Jody yelled from her side of the loft.

"OK? I'm great! That was awesome! Look out, here I come!" And she pushed off again and swung back to where Jody sat with her heart in her throat.

"Jode! That was the best! I forgot how fun it was! You've got to go next!"

"I don't know, Mare. It looks scary! I can't believe we used to do this! What if I lose my grip?" Jody asked nervously, peering down at the floor below.

"You're not going to lose your grip, there's a big old knot to hold onto. And look, the floor is covered with loose hay—even if you did fall, it would be a nice cushy landing," Mary insisted. "And besides, you're not going to fall! Come on, milking will be over soon, and we've got to go watch Star with the cows. Just do it once, that's all."

Jody tentatively took the knot in her hands and stood shakily on the edge of the hay. "Oooohhh," she whimpered just once but then closed her eyes tight and stepped off into thin air. The problem was, Jody didn't *push* off the bale, she *stepped* off the bale, so she didn't get enough momentum to really *swing* across the barn. Instead she sort of *glided* across the barn, and with her eyes shut tight, she couldn't see the bales coming up on the other side, so she didn't put her feet out in front of her for a good landing on *top* of the stack. So she ended up smacking face first into the *side* of the stack instead!

The instant Jody hit the wall of straw, her hands flew off the rope and clutched for something to hold onto. Her fingers found a grip on the strings of the top bale on the stack, and one foot stuck into the space between two bales below her.

Mary watched all this with her hand clamped over her mouth, but she recovered in time to shout instructions to Jody. "Hold on, Jode. You're OK! I'm coming over! I'm climbing down right now! I'll help you get down! Don't be scared! Just hold onto that bale and stick your other foot into that crack between the bales! Then you can't fall!" Mary had read in a book once that you should keep talking to someone in trouble, and she chattered all the way down her side of the loft and all the way up the other side where Jody hung motionless. By the time she scrambled up the stack of straw to Jody's side, she was out of breath.

"Now, Jode, it's easy to get down from here," she wheezed.

"Mary, I'm afraid to let go," Jody whispered, her eyes still squeezed shut.

"Ok, now first, let me get the rope out from under you," Mary said, gently pulling up on the rope to extract it from between Jody's body and the straw.

Mary squealed as she sailed through the air and across the empty space of the barn to the opposite side.

She let go of the rope, and it swung away into the open air. "Now, you have to open your eyes," Mary said firmly, "but don't look down!"

Jody slowly opened one eye and focused it on Mary's face, then opened the other.

"Now, just look at me, and loosen up your grip a little on the straw. You have to use your hands and feet to climb down. Come on, Jode, we do this all the time! Take a deep breath. You're not that far from the floor."

Mary clutched her own straw bale with her left hand and grasped Jody's arm firmly with her right. Jody tentatively pulled one foot from between the bales and lowered herself slowly to find a second foothold in the straw below, and moved her hands down one at a time, clutching each bale tightly as she went down. Mary moved along with her, encouraging her the whole way.

"That's it, just a little further, keep going, don't give up, we're almost there," Mary chattered relentlessly as the girls carefully descended the stack of straw. When their feet finally touched down, they collapsed in unison in a relieved heap on the loose hay covering the barn floor. Mary, of course, wasted no time in telling Jody exactly what she did wrong.

"Now, Jody, next time you get ready to swing, you have to push off hard. Then you'll make it to the other side, no problem," Mary instructed.

"I don't think there's going to be a next time, at least for a while," Jody said breathlessly. "I think I like it right here on the floor."

"Listen!" Mary said, holding up her hand for emphasis. "I think I just heard the barnyard door sliding open. Willie's letting the cows out! Let's go!" She grabbed Jody's hand and pulled her up from the barn floor, and the girls took off running out of the barn and down the barn hill toward the pasture field.

The cows were just making their slow plodding way out of the barnyard when the breathless girls reached the gate of the pasture. Star was still grazing peacefully next to Lady, and Gypsy was a little way off, dozing under the old weeping willow tree. The cows continued walking in a deliberate line along the well-worn narrow dirt path leading from the barnyard through the center of the pasture. According to habit, the cows would stay on the path until they were all out of the barnyard, and then they would spread out across the pasture to graze.

"Look, Jody, Star doesn't even see them yet. He's still just munching away, happy to be next to Lady again," Mary observed.

Just at that instant, a green-headed horsefly landed on Star's right hind leg, and he kicked out to get it off. But horseflies are known to be stubborn, and when that didn't work, Star lifted his leg and twisted his head around as far as it would go so he could bite the fly off. It was then that he saw the cows. Forgetting about the bothersome fly, he stood completely still with his leg in the air, his body bent almost in half, and stared.

Mary and Jody had to cover their mouths with their hands to keep from laughing out loud. "How long do you think he can stay like that?" Jody whispered, giggling through her fingers.

The answer came quickly as Star threw up his head in surprise and lost his balance, almost falling on his haunches. Mary and Jody giggled uncontrollably as they watched him shake his head and snort, his nostrils flaring red like a wild horse's. He extended his muzzle toward the ponderous cows as if picking up their scent, stomped his foot, and whinnied low in his throat. Lady and Gypsy, having seen the herd every day, had no reaction to them whatsoever, and the cows, who never really got excited about anything at all, didn't even notice the curious colt sniffing in their direction as they continued their trek down the dirt path.

But Star wasn't one to be ignored. As his curiosity got the better of him, he took a few tentative steps toward the last cow on the path. The cow kept walking. Star walked a little faster. The cow ignored him. Star stepped onto the path directly behind the cow and extended the tip of his inquisitive nose until it almost touched her tail. The cow didn't even give him a glance. He walked a little faster, almost a trot, and reached out and nipped the cow on the very top of her tailbone. Still no response from the cow. This was too much for Star. Trotting off the path, he positioned himself close to the cow's head and did a little buck and whinny, as if to say, "Hey, I'm over here! Look at me!"

The cow stopped. Star stopped. The cow turned her head and looked at Star. Star stared back. Then the cow, opening her mouth wide, shook her head and produced a very loud "MOOOOOO" only inches from Star's face.

Star did fall back on his haunches this time, in shock from a sound he had never heard before, at least not this close up. Mary and Jody fell on their own haunches laughing as Star recovered from his tumble and took off racing across the pasture, bucking and kicking and snorting like a wild thing while the cow continued on her leisurely trip along the packed dirt path.

"Well, I guess now we know how he's going to react to the cows," Jody giggled, picking herself up from the grass and pulling Mary up by the hand. "We'd better catch him and take him back over to the paddock before Mr. McMurray comes out and yells at us."

"Hay burner! Dead weight! Eatin' up my profits, he is!" Mary perfectly imitated Mr. McMurray's Irish brogue as the girls, holding their sides from laughing, skipped across the pasture to round up the frisky colt.

Trapped!

S TAR WAS STILL frisking about, tossing his head, and trotting in place as Mary and Jody led him through the doorway of Lucky Foot Stable after his introduction to the cows in the big pasture. He snorted so loudly just inside the little barn that Colonel Sanders squawked and flapped his wings indignantly, prompting Star to shake his head and even strike out with his forefoot in the Colonel's direction.

"Now, you calm down, boy, and mind your manners," Jody admonished him with a slight jerk on the lead rope before she released him into his stall. "Your adventures are over for one day."

"What adventures?" Willie asked, leaning over the bottom half of the Dutch door that led from the paddock into the stable.

"Willie!" yelped Mary. "You scared me! You're always appearing out of nowhere!"

"Out of nowhere? I just came from the barnyard. That's somewhere, ain't it? And what's this about an adventure?"

"Well, it wasn't really an adventure, but when you let the cows out after milking, Star met one for the first time, and she mooed at him, and he got so scared that he took off galloping and bucking across the pasture, and it was so funny!" Jody said all in one breath.

"And, Willie, you were right about Lady and Star," Mary added. "After awhile, they were getting along fine. And when we took Star out of the pasture, he didn't even make a fuss. And neither did she."

"Well, I coulda told ya that. And when you let him back out there tomorrow, they'll be fine again. But the ornery bugger will probably have to fool with the cows a couple more times before he'll be satisfied. Just don't let him chase them, or Mr. McMurray might get his shotgun after him," Willie said ominously.

"Oh, Willie, he wouldn't do that!" Jody paused. "Would he?"

"Never know. I saw him shoot in the air one time to scare some kids that were in the cornfield stealin' corn. He might just take better aim if Star chases the cows. It'll spoil their milk if they start runnin' around crazy."

"Oh, we won't let him chase them, Willie. We'll stay right out there with him for the next few days and make sure," Mary promised.

Willie walked over to Star's stall and reached a gnarly hand over the top board to scratch him between the ears while he ate his grain. "Ornery bugger," he said once more, "you better not be hollerin' to your mama and wakin' me up tonight. I got to get up earlier than usual."

"I don't think he will, Willie. She put him in his place pretty good, like you said she would," Jody said. "Now they just act like any other two horses out in a field together."

"Why do you have to get up earlier than usual, Willie?" Mary asked curiously.

"Got a load of calves goin' out before sunup," Willie said, and without further explanation, he turned and walked out the door of the stable.

"I wonder where the calves are going?" Mary asked, but Jody was too busy combing Star's unruly black and white mane to think about the calves.

"Mary, do you think we should keep Star in his stall tonight or turn him out in the paddock?" she wondered, tugging on a particularly stubborn tangle with the mane comb.

"Well, if we keep him in, he'll have a lot more energy to get rid of in the morning when we turn him out with Lady, and he might bother the cows again. It's going to be a nice night, no rain," Mary said, surveying the cloudless sky. "I vote to turn him out in the paddock. And besides, then we won't have to clean his stall tomorrow!"

"That settles it," Jody giggled.

Jody gave Star's mane one last pass with the comb and smoothed down his forelock, and with a gentle pat on his neck, she led him out to the paddock, checked to make sure his water bucket was full, and turned him loose to munch on his fluffy pile of hay.

Star was lying asleep in the corner of the little paddock before sunup the next morning, his legs twitching and making running motions as he dreamed of galloping across the pasture and chasing after one of the curious black-and-white creatures he had encountered the previous day.

His tail switched involuntarily as a fly landed on his haunches and began crawling up his side, and he snorted softly to keep another one from entering his nose. A low humming sound entered his restless brain, and his ear swiveled in response. The hum became louder and then louder still, until Star imagined in his dream a whole swarm of green-headed flies landing on him, biting and teeming around his head, trying to enter his sensitive ears. Just when he could stand it no longer, he lifted his head and shook it violently to scare off the swarm.

The sight that greeted Star's surprised gaze when he opened his eyes was not a cloud of flies, but a very large and noisy silver and blue truck parked right outside his paddock with the engine running! The sides of the truck were enclosed with wooden slats and there were two wooden doors chained shut on the back. The glare of the headlights through the semi-darkness revealed the figure of Willie hobbling toward the gate. He waved at the man sitting in the truck, unfastened the rusty chain that held the paddock gate shut, and swung it wide. Star blinked in astonishment as the creaky gate swung open and

Willie waved for the truck driver to drive through the opening and into the middle of the paddock! Star clambered to his feet and backed up into the narrow space between Lucky Foot Stable and the big white dairy barn. Poking his head around the corner, he watched wide-eyed as the big truck turned in a tight circle and backed up to the loading ramp that extended from the barnyard door of the dairy barn into the far end of the paddock.

"C'mon back, c'mon back," Willie waved the driver on until the back of the truck was just touching the packed dirt of the loading ramp. The truck driver climbed down from behind the wheel, unfastened the wooden doors at the back of the truck, and swung them open so they met the wooden sides of the ramp, making a chute leading from the barnyard door into the bed of the truck. Willie helped the driver open the little doors on the inside of the truck bed where several stalls lined either side of the enclosure, and then he hobbled down to the barnyard door and opened it.

"Hey up! Hey up!" Willie called, disappearing into the darkness of the barnyard. An instant later, Star backed even further into his corner when a group of about ten little black-and-white calves, kicking up their heels and bawling, trotted up the ramp followed by Willie, who was brandishing a stick. Into the back of the truck they went, where the driver was waiting to shut them into their stalls.

The truck driver fastened the last of the stall doors inside the truck, closed one of the big wooden truck doors, and was about to close the other when Willie spoke.

"Daggonit, I forgot to bring out their identification papers," he said, pulling on his earlobe. "If you don't mind followin' me into the barn, I'll get 'em out of the desk."

Star stood very still and watched as Willie and the driver vanished into the barnyard. Then he immediately extended his muzzle and sniffed curiously in the direction of the calves, who were still mooing and kicking the sides of their little enclosures. He took a hesitant step from his little space and approached the back of the truck tentatively. His ears were pricked up, and he sniffed and snorted all the while. In the dim light of the rising sun, he stepped onto the loading ramp and peered into the back of the truck through the one door that had been left open by the truck driver. An inquisitive calf gazed back at him and mooed softly. Star timidly took a

Star was so busy comforting all the calves in the row that he didn't hear Willie and the truck driver.

few more steps up the ramp until he was close enough to sniff noses with the confused calf. Upon seeing Star, the other calves began mooing at him as if he were their long lost mother, and he continued up and into the truck, sniffing all of their poor little noses as he went.

Star was so busy comforting all the calves in the row that he didn't hear Willie and the truck driver come out of the barn. The next sound he heard was the wooden door on the back of the truck slamming shut!

"Almost forgot to shut that door," the truck driver chuckled to Willie. "You know, one time I did forget it, and two heifers jumped out on the road. That's one reason I built the stalls in there. That way, if I forget to shut the door, they ain't gonna jump out. And it's easier on them for the trip, instead of bein' all jostled up in one group."

"I know what you mean," Willie said as the driver climbed in and started the noisy engine. At the sound of Willie's voice, Star nickered softly, then more loudly as he saw Willie open the gate of the paddock for the truck driver. But the rumble of the engine drowned out the sound. The anxious colt almost lost his footing and fell as the truck lurched forward through the gate and started down the farm lane. Star peered through the slats of the thick wooden doors and saw Willie closing the paddock gate. This time he whinnied frantically, but it was no use. The noisy truck lumbered down the lane and onto the road, leaving Willie and Lucky Foot Stable far behind.

✦ 12 ✦
Where Is Star?

"LAST ONE TO Lucky Foot is a rotten egg!" Mary hollered, pedaling her bike furiously up the farm lane neck and neck with Jody. The girls rode their bikes to the farm each morning from their homes at opposite ends of the road, and it just so happened that this morning they had reached the long gravelly lane at the same instant. It then became a race to see who would reach the stable first. Skidding to a stop in front of the white wooden doors at precisely the same moment, the race was declared a dead heat.

"It's a tie!" Jody yelled, wiping her sweaty forehead with the sleeve of her T-shirt. "No rotten eggs!" she giggled.

Mary propped her bike up on its kickstand and opened the stable door. "Hello, Walter. Good day, Colonel Sanders," she greeted the birds roosting on the top board of Lady's stall. "How ever are you this morning?" The Colonel responded by shaking his head and ruffling his feathers, while Walter just sat and cocked his head sideways.

"Mare, I had an idea when I woke up this morning," Jody declared. "Why don't we put Star's saddle and bridle on and try longeing him? My dad gave me that longe line for my birthday, and I've never tried it. I bet he would learn really fast!"

"Excellent idea!" Mary agreed. "Let's bring him in and feed him first, and then we'll get started."

Mary and Jody went to the Dutch door leading into the paddock and looked over. "Star!" Mary called. "Come in, come in, we're going to learn something new today!"

"Star?" Jody called again, looking around the empty paddock. "Where are you?"

"Hmph," Mary exclaimed, "he must be hiding back in his little corner."

"That's weird," Jody replied. "He's always right here waiting for us in the morning." She opened the bottom of the Dutch door and walked to the narrow space between Lucky Foot Stable and the big white dairy barn, where Star sometimes liked to hide.

"Mare, he's not here," she said worriedly, peering into the space and then around the paddock again as if hoping Star would miraculously appear from thin air. "Where could he be?"

"Maybe Willie came and got him after milking and turned him out in the pasture again with Lady and Gypsy," Mary offered. "Maybe he wanted to see how he would act with the cows today, and he didn't want to wait for us," she continued, not sounding at all sure that Willie would do any such thing. The girls stared at each other for an instant, and then in unison they turned and took off at a gallop toward the pasture.

Before they reached the pasture gate, Mary and Jody could see Lady and Gypsy grazing peacefully under the old weeping willow tree. Star, however, was nowhere to be seen—not playing among the cows, not near the barnyard door, and not by the little stream that meandered aimlessly through the pasture and into the woods. The girls stood and stared mutely at the scene before them until Mary found her voice.

"We've got to find Willie," she said confidently. "I bet Star got out of the paddock, and he's wandering around the farm somewhere, probably up by the chicken house. Oh, I hope he didn't get into the grain room! He'll eat himself sick!" And with that, the girls took off at a dead run toward the big stone house where Mr. McMurray lived.

Mary and Jody were gasping for air when they reached the old farmhouse, but they knocked frantically on the stout screen door without even stopping to catch their breath. In a moment Mrs. McMurray appeared and looked down at the red-faced girls in surprise.

"What's all this, then?" she asked, pushing the screen door open with a squeak. "What's happened?"

"Mrs. McMurray," panted Mary, "is Willie here? Did he come in for breakfast yet?"

"Why, sure he has, he's come and gone," Mrs. McMurray replied. "He doesn't stay long, you know. Always too much to do. Now what's the trouble?"

"Oh, Mrs. McMurray, have you seen Star? Has he been up here wandering around the chicken yard or anything?" Jody asked. "He's not in his paddock, and we don't know where he's gone."

"Star? You mean the baby?" Mrs. McMurray asked, wiping her hands on her apron. Mary and Jody nodded hopefully.

"No, I haven't seen him around this way. How could he get out of the paddock? Was the gate left open? Or the stable door?"

Mary and Jody looked at each other. They hadn't thought to check how Star may have gotten out of the paddock. But they knew the gate was closed, and so was the stable door.

"We don't know, ma'am," Jody said tearfully, "but he's gone and we have to find Willie!"

"Well, I think he went home for a few minutes. He usually does right after breakfast. You should check there."

Before Mrs. McMurray had finished her sentence, Mary and Jody flew off in the direction of the farm's little tenant house, where Willie lived. They ran up the gravel driveway, leapt onto the porch, and began pounding furiously on the wooden frame of the screen door.

"Willie!" Mary yelled, after knocking for only a few seconds without a reply. "Willie, are you in there? It's Mary and Jody—we need you!"

"I'm here, I'm here. What do you want?" Willie called grumpily from somewhere in the back of the house.

"Willie, can you come out? We need you!" Jody repeated.

"Hold yer horses, I'll be out in a minute. Come in if you want to."

The girls pushed open the screen door and stood just inside the tiny living room of Willie's house, fidgeting and biting their fingernails as they waited for Willie. Mary began pacing around the room in a circle while Jody looked nervously through the screen as if expecting Star to come trotting up the walk at any moment.

Suddenly Mary stopped pacing. She stood still and stared at a collection of framed photographs on an end table by Willie's tattered easy chair. Picking up one of the photos, she peered at it more closely, her mouth open in shock.

"Jody!" she exclaimed in a stage whisper. "Come here!"

"What?" Jody asked, annoyed that Mary could be distracted by anything during the current crisis.

"Look at this!" Mary continued, holding the photo

up for Jody to see. "It's Willie," she said, pointing to a handsome young man in a group of men on horseback, "on a horse. In uniform! He must've been in the army or something!"

Jody picked up another of the photos—this one of Willie with a man in a ten-gallon hat and a bandana around his neck. At the bottom of the photo was an inscription. Jody wiped the dust from the glass and squinted to read it. "Look at this, Mare, it says, 'To Will: thanks for all your help. Good riding! John Wayne.'"

"John Wayne!" Mary squealed. "Let me see that!" She grabbed the photo from Jody's hand and held it close to her face. "Jode! It says John Wayne!"

"I know, I know," Jody said, puzzled. "Mare, who's John Wayne?"

Mary looked at Jody in disbelief. "Who's John Wayne? Jody, I can't believe you asked me that question! John Wayne, major motion picture star of all the great Westerns? Most excellent horseback rider and role model for our circus act? Don't you remember the night you came over and me and you and mom watched *True Grit?*"

"Was that the one where the horse fell down and died from exhaustion because those two people were galloping it all over without stopping?" Jody asked with a grimace. "I covered my eyes and refused to watch the rest of the movie, remember?"

"Well, yeah, that was a bad part," Mary admitted. "But that was John Wayne in the movie! And this is John Wayne in the picture with Willie! How in the world . . ."

"What's all the ruckus about?" Willie's voice came from the hallway. Jody and Mary hastily put the photos back and turned to face him as he entered the room. In the excitement of seeing the photo of John Wayne, they had almost forgotten why they had come. But at the sight of Willie, they quickly remembered.

"Willie!" they screeched in unison. "Do you know where Star is?"

"Star?" Willie asked, pulling on his earlobe. "Last time I seen him he was in his stall."

"In his stall?" Jody and Mary looked at each other. "We didn't look in his stall!" And off they flew once again, back to Lucky Foot Stable, with Willie hobbling along behind.

When Willie finally entered the stable, he was met by the sight of two blubbering girls going from

Lady's stall to Gypsy's to Star's, looking in each one as if Star would appear any minute out of nowhere.

"Willie, he's not here. He's not here," Jody wailed. "When did you put him in his stall?"

"Me, put him in his stall?" Willie asked, scratching the side of his head. "I didn't put him in his stall. You did. Yesterday afternoon."

"Oh, but we turned him out after that because it was a nice night, and we thought he would be happier outside."

"You turned him out . . ." suddenly Willie stopped scratching his head. His hand dropped to his side, and the color drained from his face. "You turned him out . . . in the paddock?"

"Yes, Willie! Last night!" Mary cried. "He was . . ." Mary stopped in mid-sentence at the stricken look on Willie's face. "Willie? Willie, what's wrong?"

"Now, now, let me just think a minute . . . he was in the paddock this mornin'. . . and . . ." Willie didn't say any more.

"Willie, what are you thinking?" Jody asked frantically. "Do you know where he is?"

"Well, now we had a load of calves go out this mornin' . . . if he was in the paddock . . . we loaded the calves in the paddock . . . up the loadin' ramp . . ."

"Well, we had a load of calves go out this mornin'. . .
If he was in the paddock . . ."

Willie looked at the girls, who stared back at him with their mouths wide open.

"Willie, where did the calves go?" Mary finally asked in a tiny voice.

Willie turned and looked at the loading ramp. He looked up at the sky. He scratched his head and pulled his earlobe. Finally he looked at the girls and winced. "Well, now, you know they were veal calves . . . raised for meat . . ."

Mary and Jody looked at each other with their mouths wide open, but no sound emerged. Then as one they found their voice.

"*WILLIE!*" they screamed.

★ 13 ★

The Slaughterhouse

WILLIE'S OLD RED pickup truck had never traveled so fast over the bumpy country road as it did now, far beyond its usual clip of twenty-five miles per hour. Willie occasionally glanced sidelong at Mary wringing her hands and Jody biting her fingernails as they jounced along in shocked silence. After the terrible knowledge had sunk in that Star had somehow gotten himself trapped with the load of calves destined for the slaughterhouse, Willie and the girls had rushed to put the old wooden sides on Willie's truck that they had built for taking Lady to her first horse show. Now the truck bed was ready for a passenger, and they each silently prayed that Star would soon be jouncing along behind them on their way home.

Willie drove in silence for a moment longer, but he had made up his mind to break the news he had been keeping to himself. *Better to let them know now,* he thought, *rather than have another surprise later on.* He tugged on his earlobe and cleared his throat.

"Now, you know," he said gently, "I'm not real sure which place that driver went to. There's a couple . . . a couple of . . . places like . . . that around these parts. I'm headin' to the one where I think he went. But if it's not this one, we'll have to turn around and try the other one."

Mary and Jody looked at Willie without saying a word. Jody's hand went slowly to her mouth and finally a sob escaped, then another, until her shoulders shook with the burden of her lament. Mary silently took the bandana from her head and offered it to Jody. When she didn't take it, Mary used it to dry her own tears while Willie drove on, stone-faced.

Rounding the next curve, Willie suddenly put on the brakes. The sign for Curran's Rendering Plant loomed ominously by the side of the road. Mary raised her head as Willie made the sharp right turn and began creeping slowly down the long gravel lane that led to the plant.

Now that they had reached their destination, Willie was in no hurry to see what they might encounter at the end of that lane.

"Ugghh, what is that smell?" Mary asked, grimacing and holding her nose. Willie glanced at her sharply, and Mary, realizing what the smell was, clapped her hand over her mouth. But it was too late. Jody's head jerked up, and she looked out the window just in time to see, past the stand of trees around the last bend in the lane and down in a hollow, an unimposing gray cinder block building. The building could have been used for almost any purpose. What made it different were the pens. Built against one side of the structure were row upon row of wooden pens. They were separated by gates, and full of livestock of all descriptions. Cows, steers, pigs, sheep, even goats bawled and bleated and grunted in a cacophony of sound. Several livestock trucks, some double-decker and built of aluminum, and others smaller, with simple wooden sides, were lined up near the pens, waiting to unload. Willie came to a full stop in the middle of the lane and the three stared at the sight below them until Mary found her voice.

"Look, there's the calf pens!" She pointed at a row of enclosures just visible on the other side of the building. Jody looked through the windshield of the truck and saw the calves milling around in the pen, bawling for their mothers, and she began to bawl herself, louder than before, her hands covering her face.

"Willie, I can't look!" she wailed. "Is Star in there? Do you see him anywhere?"

Willie crept the truck forward and patted Jody awkwardly on the arm. "Listen, now, I can't imagine they would unload him with the calves and not see he was different. As soon as they seen he was a colt and not a calf, they'd know to separate him and call the farm. I'm just lookin' for that truck and driver that picked him up, and I don't see them any-wheres."

Then it was Mary's turn to wail. "Oh, Willie, you mean he might be at the other place? How far away is it? Can we just drive down closer to the pens and look to be sure? Maybe he's in there and we can't see him! Or maybe the truck is around the other side of the building!" she babbled.

"I'm goin,' I'm goin,'" Willie said, drifting down the hill toward the calf pens.

"Oh, Willie, he must be so scared!" Jody lamented. "And confused—he's probably wondering why we haven't rescued him yet! Oh, please let him be here," she prayed.

Willie drove down to the calf pens and around the other side of the building and even near the holding pens for the larger livestock, but Star was nowhere to be seen. Just as they made one more pass, a man appeared by the front of the building, walking toward the cow pens. Willie stopped the truck and waved to him. The man waved back and approached the truck.

"Mornin,'" Willie greeted the man nonchalantly as if nothing was amiss.

"Mornin,' sir," the man replied cordially. "What can I do for you? Nothin' in the back of the truck, I see."

"No, no, not today," Willie chuckled, taking off his hat and scratching the side of his head. Mary and Jody wiggled impatiently, waiting for Willie to ask about Star. He finally replaced his hat and went on, "I was just wonderin' if you've had anything out of the ordinary come in this mornin'?"

"Out of the ordinary? You mean, like a llama or something?" the man laughed.

"No, no, I was thinkin' more along the lines of a colt? A black-and-white colt—these girls lost theirs, and they think he might be here somewhere," Willie chuckled again.

The man started to laugh, but when he glanced in the truck and saw the stricken faces of the two girls, he stopped and shook his head. "No, can't say I've seen anything like that today," he said gravely. "But if I hear tell of a lost colt in the vicinity, I'll be sure to get in touch with you," he continued. "What farm are you with?"

"McMurray's dairy," Willie replied. "He ships calves here a few times a year. We think the colt might have got mixed in with the shipment some-how, ornery bugger that he is."

"Well, I don't know of a shipment coming from there today, but then the boss doesn't tell me every-thing. And he's not here right now to ask about it. You might want to try going down the road to Gardner's."

"Yep, that's our next stop," Willie said. "Thank you for your time."

Mary and Jody waited for Willie to drive a good

distance up the road before they turned to him and moaned in unison, "Willie!"

"What?" Willie asked. "I'm drivin' as fast as I can. We'll get over to Gardner's, and Star will be there waitin' for us. He must be there, if he ain't here," he continued, trying to sound confident for the girl's sake.

"But what if he's not?" Mary worried. "How can you be so calm, and even laughing with that man and everything? Star could be . . ."

"Whoa!" Willie exclaimed suddenly. He turned almost completely around in his seat, and then he slammed on the brakes.

"What? What is it, Willie?" Jody yelled.

But Willie was too busy making a sudden turn in the middle of the road to reply. The old truck almost went up on two wheels as Willie spun it around and stepped on the gas like a teenager. Mary and Jody grabbed hands and the dashboard to keep from being flung against the passenger door.

"Willie! What in the world . . ." Mary shrieked. Then she peered over the dashboard to see a blue and silver truck with wooden sides on the road ahead of them, heading in the direction of the slaughterhouse.

If I hear tell of a lost colt in the vicinity, I'll be sure
to get in touch with you," he continued.

"Willie! Is that the truck? Is that where Star is?" Jody implored.

"That's the truck," Willie said, stone-faced. "Lucky I seen it when it passed by. Whether Star is in there, that I don't know. But I reckon we'll find out."

"Willie! Blow your horn! Make him stop!" Mary yelled, tugging frantically on Willie's arm.

"He'll stop soon enough when he gets to the plant," Willie said. "I'll talk to him then."

Mary and Jody wanted to fling open the truck door and chase the truck down the road in the few minutes it took to arrive back at the plant. Instead they squinted through the dusty windshield, desperately trying to get a glimpse of Star through the narrow slats in the heavy wooden doors at the rear of the truck. Even Willie found himself leaning over the steering wheel, narrowing his eyes and swerving slightly in the road to try and get a better look. But Star was nowhere to be seen.

★ 14 ★
The Rescue

WHEN AT LAST the big truck rumbled down the slope and into the livestock yard, Mary and Jody could wait no longer. Flinging open the door of the old red pickup the second Willie put his foot on the brake, the girls fell all over each other in their haste to run over and see Star.

"Hey!" Willie yelled in his sternest voice. "Hey, I said. You just stop right there."

From the tone of Willie's voice, the girls knew he expected to be obeyed. They stopped in their tracks and turned to him with imploring looks.

"You two wait right here. You can't just go runnin' up to that man, scarin' him half to death. I'll see what's goin' on, and then when I say, you can come over."

"But, Willie . . ." Mary began.

"No arguin,'" Willie insisted. "And no movin' from that spot."

The real purpose of Willie's scolding was to prevent the girls from seeing something they may not want to see in the back of the truck, and Willie was feeling a little nervous himself as he hobbled over to speak with the truck driver. Mary and Jody linked arms and jiggled anxiously by the pickup, watching Willie gesture toward the back of the livestock truck. The driver shook his head, and together he and Willie walked back and peered through the slats of the thick wooden doors. After what seemed an eternity to the two distraught girls, Willie beckoned for them to come and see for themselves.

What Mary and Jody saw when the truck driver finally swung open the right back door and they squinted into the dim interior of the truck was a miserable weanling colt with his head hanging down and his front legs splayed for balance, trembling in fear in a back corner while the calves bawled all around him. At the sight of the two girls, he raised his head a little and managed a weak nicker.

"Well, I'll be . . ." the driver mumbled, looking incredulously from Star to the agitated girls.

"Star! Oh, poor Star!" they exclaimed together while trying to find some way to climb into the high bed of the truck.

"Now, just hold yer horses," Willie said gruffly. "We got to back up to the loadin' ramp to get him out of there. He ain't gonna jump out, is he?"

"Oh, hurry, Willie, he wants to come home!"

So the truck was backed up to the ramp, and the doors opened once more. Mary and Jody stood anxiously at the bottom of the ramp while Willie stepped into the bed of the truck, lead rope in hand, whirring softly in his throat as he approached the frightened colt.

"Hey, little buddy," he said soothingly. "You ornery little bugger. You got yourself in trouble this time, didn't you?"

Star extended his muzzle and sniffed at Willie's outstretched hand, nickered low in his throat, and took a tentative step forward. Willie snapped the lead rope onto his halter and scratched gently

The girls were laughing and crying all at the same time as they wrapped their arms around Star's neck.

between his ears while Star rubbed his head up and down, up and down on Willie's arm.

"Willie! Can you bring him out? Is he still too scared?" Jody asked in a whisper.

"We're comin,' we're comin,' Willie said brusquely, clearing his throat and rubbing a gnarly hand across his eyes before turning to face the girls. As he turned to lead Star from the truck, the cantankerous colt pushed him with his muzzle as if to say, "Let's get out of here, quick!"

"Daggone ornery bugger!" Willie exclaimed as he led Star down the ramp and into the hands of the two girls, who were laughing and crying all at the same time as they wrapped their arms around Star's neck and kissed the end of his nose. He reciprocated by snorting wetly in their faces, sending them into a fit of giggles.

"All right, now, enough of this foolishness. I got to get back in time for milkin,'" Willie insisted. "You girls hold him right here, and I'll back the truck up to the ramp. Then we just gotta hope he'll get in."

It almost seemed as if Star knew he was going home as Willie led him easily onto the thick layer of straw covering the bed of the truck. Willie tied him with a slip knot, and he immediately dropped his head to munch on the pile of hay the girls had arranged for him. After giving him one last grateful pat, Mary and Jody helped secure the back doors of the makeshift trailer and climbed wearily into the old red pickup. They were on their way home at last.

★ 15 ★
Manners

MARY AND JODY spent that evening and the whole next day fawning over Star—grooming him, giving him extra sugar cubes and carrots, fluffing up the bed of straw in his stall, and making sure he had plenty of good green hay. Neither girl would leave his side for a moment. Of course, Star responded to the special treatment by acting like a spoiled celebrity. He stretched up his muzzle and knocked Colonel Sanders off his perch. Then he reached over and lipped at the latch on his stall door until he almost got it open. Just after the girls fluffed and arranged his bed of straw just so, Star pawed at it, flung it all over, lay down, and rolled. And when Jody brought a scoop of grain into the stall to dump into his manger, he brazenly knocked it out of her hand! It was just at that moment that Willie entered Lucky Foot Stable.

"What in the . . ." Willie exclaimed when he saw the grain go flying. Then Star used his head to push Jody out of the stall door and stamped his foot as if to say, "Get out now and leave me alone!" At that, Willie strode to the front of the stall, clapped once, and deep in his throat gave warning.

"Hey, now. You settle down and behave yourself," he growled. Star threw up his head and looked curiously at Willie. Upon seeing the stern expression on the farmhand's face, his ears swiveled back, and he lowered his head as if ashamed of himself. Then Willie turned to Mary and Jody, who stood right outside the stall with their mouths hanging open.

"Shut your mouths and listen to me," he began. "You two are spoiling this colt rotten, and he's just gonna take advantage of you until he gets out of control."

"But Willie," Jody began, "he had such a hard day yesterday . . ."

"No, I noticed last week how he was startin' to push you around," Willie interrupted, "and spoilin' him even more now just because he had a hard day ain't gonna do him any good. Raisin' a colt is just like raisin' a human. They need guidelines and discipline, or you got yourself a good-for-nothin' . . ."

"But he does behave most of the time. He lets us put his saddle and bridle on, and he doesn't bite or kick . . ." Mary insisted.

"That's all well and good, and it's good to praise him when he behaves, but when he acts up, you got to let him know it's wrong, or he'll think anything he does is OK with you," Willie explained.

The girls stood quietly and let this information sink in. "But Willie," Jody finally asked, "what do we do? We can't beat him. He'll hate us! And we could never do that anyway!"

"I didn't say nothin' about anybody beatin' anybody," Willie snorted. "There's ways to train a colt without that. Now if we can get him in shape, we might . . ." Willie stopped in mid-sentence.

"We might what, Willie?" Mary asked curiously. "What?"

"Well, I wasn't goin' to say nothin,' seein' as how you girls are gonna bug me to death," Willie continued.

"Say nothin' about what?" Jody asked.

"Well," Willie said, tugging on his earlobe, "I was talkin' to that truck driver yesterday for a minute after we got Star loaded up. He was sayin' what a right nice lookin' colt he is."

"Of course, he's a nice looking colt! He's gorgeous!" said Jody proudly.

"But I mean a good show colt," Willie continued. "The man raises quarter horses and he holds a show at his place twice a year. He has halter classes and everything—for all breeds."

"Halter classes? What's that mean?" Mary asked.

"It means that you show your animal in hand, not saddled up or anything, and he's judged on his conformation, his trueness to the breed, the way he handles, and his *manners,*" Willie put a lot of emphasis on the word manners, glaring at Star as he did so. "They have classes for yearlings."

Willie's meaning slowly began to sink in with the two girls. "His conformation, Willie? Does that mean how he looks?" Jody asked excitedly, looking proudly at Star.

"How he's put together. And I guess you could say that little cuss is put together pretty well," Willie admitted, smiling at Star in spite of himself before turning sternly to Mary and Jody.

"But if you keep spoilin' him rotten, he won't be good for nothin' but the meat truck."

"Willie! Don't say that! We won't spoil him rotten anymore. You'll have to help us. We'll get him ready for the show, and he'll be the best paint colt anybody has ever seen!" Mary exaggerated.

"Well, we've got some time to work with him," Willie said. "Show won't be for another six months or so. Now I gotta go fix fence." And as abruptly as Willie had entered the little stable, he turned to go.

"Willie! Wait!" Jody called, just as he reached the door. When Willie turned back, Jody clamped her mouth shut and turned beet red.

"What? I don't have time for any more foolishness."

"I want to read something to you. And you too, Mare. I wrote it last night after we rescued Star."

"It's a poem! A poem, I bet. Willie, did you know Jody was a great poet?" Mary asked proudly.

"A great poet? No, I never heard nothin' about that," Willie said, shaking his head. "But if there's any poetry to be heard, let's hear it, 'cause I got to put up a fence board before I turn the cows out of the barnyard," he continued kindly, noticing Jody's embarrassment.

Jody took a piece of paper from her pocket and shook it out, trying to smooth the wrinkles against her jeans.

Mary went on, "Willie, you never even heard Jody's Christmas poem! It was great, and she's going to write a whole collection of poems and get them published, and then she'll be rich and famous and buy a farm just for Lady and Gypsy and Star! And me, of course," she said smugly.

Willie said nothing as he stood waiting patiently for Jody to begin her poem.

"This isn't like the Christmas poem, Mary—it's funnier. So it's OK to laugh." And she cleared her throat and began to read:

> *Star of Wonder is very bright,*
> *Except when he sees a curious sight.*
> *Then due to his curiosity,*
> *He sticks his nose where it shouldn't be!*
> *He walked up the ramp and got in the truck,*
> *And before he knew it, he soon was stuck.*
> *Riding with calves who were meeting their fate,*
> *We were so afraid we would be too late!*
> *But Willie drove fast and saved the day,*

And Star is back home. Hooray! Hooray!
Now we can't let him out of our sight,
We'll watch him morning, noon, and night!
'Cause the minute we look the other way,
The ornery bugger might run away!

Jody looked up from reading her poem in time to see Willie take off his hat, scratch the side of his head, and after passing a weathered hand across his eyes, turn and walk from the stable.

"Uh, oh, Mary, I don't think Willie liked the poem. He didn't say anything!" Jody worried, going to the stable door as if ready to follow Willie out to the field.

"No, Jode, I think Willie liked it. I think he liked it a lot," Mary said quietly. "I bet nobody has ever written a poem with him in it before. You should have seen his face when you were reading it. I think he liked it so much, he couldn't say a word."

Jody sighed with contentment, and walking over to Star's stall, she opened the door and went in, holding the wrinkled paper up for Star to see.

"How did you like it, buddy?" she asked. Star responded by taking the paper in his teeth and

When he raised his head, the poem was torn perfectly
in two, one half still in his teeth.

ripping it from Jody's hand. Then he turned to the back corner of the stall, lowered his nose to the ground, and stepped on half of the paper with his front hoof. When he raised his head, the poem was torn perfectly in two, one half still in his teeth. Star shook the scrap of paper up and down, up and down, snorting and stomping his foot all the while. Mary and Jody speechlessly watched the frisky colt, then looked at each other. And in that moment they agreed without a word that the training of Star of Wonder must soon begin in earnest.

Glossary of Horse Terms

Bale—In stable terms, a bale is a closely packed bundle of either hay or straw (see definitions) measuring about two by three feet, weighing about forty pounds, and tied with two strings lengthwise. When the strings are cut, the bale can be shaken loose and can be used either as feed, in the case of hay, or as stall bedding, in the case of straw.

Baling twine—The term used for the thick yellow string that is tied around a bale.

Bank barn—A barn that is built into the side of a hill so that the hill forms a "ramp" leading into the upper part of the barn, where hay and straw may be stored; the bottom floor of the barn is used for milking cows if it is a dairy barn, or it may have stalls for the purpose of sheltering other animals.

Barn swallow—A small, blue-black bird with a rusty-colored breast and throat and a forked tail; found all over North America and Europe, these friendly birds like to build their nests in barns and eat insects.

Bay—A common coloring seen in horses and ponies. The body is reddish-brown with black mane, tail, and lower legs.

Bit—The metal piece on the bridle inserted into the mouth of a horse that provides communication between the rider and horse.

Blinders—A leather attachment to a driving bridle designed to restrict the vision of a horse from the rear and sides, and to focus the vision forward.

Breeching straps—An attachment to the driving harness that fits across the hindquarters of the horse about twelve inches below the dock of the tail and fastens to the shafts of the cart. These straps help to keep the cart from hitting the horse when going down a hill.

Bridle—The leather headgear, with a metal bit, which is placed on the head of a horse to enable the rider to control the horse.

Canter—A three-beat gait of a horse, which can also be called a "collected gallop." It is slightly faster than a trot, and not so "bouncy."

Carriage—A horse-drawn, four-wheeled vehicle.

Carriage robe—A heavy blanket about five feet square, which is used to cover the legs of the occupant of a carriage or sleigh and provide warmth while riding.

Chestnut—A common coloring found in horses and ponies. The coat is basically red, in varying shades on different horses. The mane and tail are the same color as the body.

Cluck—The "clicking" sound a rider or driver makes from the corner of the mouth to urge a horse forward. Also the sound a chicken makes when communicating.

Collar—The oval, leather piece of harness that fits around the horse's neck, and to which the hames and traces are attached. The collar allows the horse to pull the carriage by pushing his weight against the collar and walking forward.

Corncob—The inner segment of an ear of corn to which the corn kernels are attached. The horse eats the kernels but not the cob.

Crop—A short leather riding whip carried by the rider and used lightly to encourage the horse to move forward.

Crosstie—The method of tying a horse squarely in the aisle or stall by clipping a rope to both sides of the halter. When a horse is crosstied, he cannot move away from the rider during grooming and saddling.

Crupper—The part of the driving harness that fastens around the top of the tail to help keep the saddle and breeching straps in place.

Dismount—The action of getting down from a horse and onto the ground.

Dock—The bone in a horse's tail, formed of the lowest vertebrae of the spine.

Dollar bareback—A game played on horseback, in which a dollar is placed under the knee of the rider while riding bareback and the riders must walk, trot, and even canter around the ring without losing the dollar. The last person with the dollar still under his knee wins all the dollars.

Eaves—The overhanging lower edge of a roof.

Field horse—Another term for a work horse; that is, a horse that is hitched to and performs work in a field, such as plowing or planting.

Flake—A section of hay that is taken from a bale for feeding, usually about six inches wide and two feet square. There are usually about ten flakes of hay in a whole bale.

Flaxen—A type of coloring sometimes found on chestnut horses, and always found on palominos, in which the mane and tail are white. If a chestnut has a flaxen mane and tail, he is known as a "flaxen chestnut."

Foal—A young, unweaned horse or pony of either gender. When the horse or pony is "weaned," or separated from its mother, it is called a "weanling."

Gallop—A fast, four-beat gait in which all four of the horse's feet strike the ground separately.

Grain—Harvested cereals or other edible seeds, including oats, corn, wheat, and barley. Horses and ponies often eat a mixture of grains, vitamins, minerals, and molasses called "sweet feed."

Gray—A common color found in horses and ponies. A gray horse is born black and gradually lightens with age from a steel-gray color to almost white.

Graze—Eat grass. Horses and ponies will graze continually when turned out on good pasture.

Groom—To groom a horse is to clean and brush his coat, comb his mane and tail, and pick the dirt from his hooves. A person known as a "groom" goes along on a horse show or horse race to help with grooming, tacking up, or anything else that needs to be done.

Ground drive—The act of driving a horse in full harness but not hooked to a cart or carriage. A person steers the horse by walking behind the horse and holding the long reins. This is a method used to train a horse to drive.

Gully—A trench worn in the earth by running water after a rain.

Gymkhana—A horse show made up of games played on horseback, including games defined elsewhere in this glossary.

Halter—Also known as a "head collar," a halter is made of rope, leather, or nylon and is placed on the head of a horse and used for leading or tying him. The halter has no bit, but it has a metal ring that rests under the chin of the horse to which you attach a lead rope.

Hames—The metal pieces of the driving harness that fasten around the collar and are attached to the traces.

Hard brush—A grooming tool resembling a scrub brush, usually with firm bristles made of nylon, used to brush dried mud or dirt from the coat and legs of a horse or pony.

Harness—The collection of leather straps, bridle, reins, and collar that is placed on a horse or pony and attached to a cart, sleigh, or carriage.

Haunches—Another term for the hindquarters of a horse or pony.

Hay—Grass or other herbage that is cut in the field and allowed to dry over several days, then usually baled and stored in the barn to feed to animals.

Haynet—A nylon or rope net that is stuffed with loose hay and tied at the top, then hung in a stall or trailer to allow an animal to eat from it.

Hindquarters—The rear of a horse or pony, including the back legs.

Hitch up—Attach a horse or pony to a cart, carriage, or sleigh through the use of the harness straps.

Hoof pick—A grooming tool used to clean dirt and gravel from the hooves of a horse of pony.

Hooves—The hard covering of the foot of a horse or pony. The hooves must be cleaned before and after riding and trimmed every six weeks (or so) to keep them from growing too long.

Jump standards—The wooden or vinyl upright supports on either side of the jump that hold the jump cups onto which the jump rails or poles are placed.

Keyhole race—A game played on horseback, in which a pattern in the shape of a keyhole is painted or limed on the ground and the rider gallops the horse or pony to the end of the pattern and back again without stepping outside the lines. The fastest time wins.

Lead rope—A short (about six feet) length of cotton or nylon rope with a snap attached to the end. The rope is used to lead the horse or pony.

Leg up—The action of helping someone mount by grasping their bended left knee and hoisting them up and onto the back of the horse or pony.

Leather conditioner—An oily or creamy substance that is rubbed into leather to help keep it from drying out.

Lines—Another term for the long reins used with a harness to drive a horse.

Loft—The large area in the top of a barn used to store bales of hay and straw.

Mane—The long hair that grows on the crest (top) of a horse's or pony's neck.

Manger—A wooden box with an open top, usually attached to the wall of the stall, used for feeding grain to a horse or pony.

Mare—A female horse or pony three years of age or older.

Mare's tails—Also known as cirrus clouds, these are wispy cloud formations that actually look like the long flowing tail of a horse or pony.

Milkers—The equipment that is attached to the cow's teats in order to draw the milk out through a pulsing action.

Milk house—The small building attached to the dairy barn where the milk ends up in a cooling tank.

Mustang—A native breed of horse that is found mostly in the western plains and lives in the wild, although many mustangs have been caught and tamed for riding.

Muzzle—The lower end of the nose of a horse or pony, which includes the nostrils, lips, and chin.

Neat's-foot oil—A type of oil used to condition leather to keep it from drying out.

Nicker—A low, quiet sound made by a horse or pony in greeting or when wanting to be fed.

Obstacle course—A game played on horseback involving various obstacles that the rider and horse or pony must maneuver, such as going over a bridge, trotting between poles, opening gates while mounted, etc.

Paddock—A fenced area, smaller than a field, used for enclosing animals for limited exercise.

Pinto—A horse or pony of a solid coat color with white patches or markings on various parts of the body. The mane and tail may be various colors.

Pole bending—A game played on horseback that involves riding a horse or pony through a slalom pattern in and out of vertical poles without touching the poles. Fastest times wins.

Pony—A pony measures below 14.3 hands from the bottom of the hoof to the withers. (See definition.) A hand equals four inches. An animal 14.3 hands or above is considered a horse.

Reins—The leather straps of the bridle attached to the bit and held by the rider to guide and control the horse.

Ringmaster—The person at a horse show who assists the judge in the ring and helps any rider who falls; this person may also replace any rails that are knocked down on jumps.

Saddle—A padded leather seat for a rider, placed on a horse's or pony's back and secured by a girth. A harness placed on the horse's or pony's back behind the withers is also called a saddle.

Saddlebags—Two leather pouches attached to each other by a wide piece of leather that drapes over the saddle or withers of the horse, or sometimes behind the saddle, to allow the rider to carry supplies on the trail.

Saddle rack—A metal or wooden frame in the shape of a saddle attached to the wall or stall, on which to hang the saddle.

Salt block—A square, compact brick of salt placed in the field or stall for a horse to lick, which provides him with salt and other necessary minerals.

Shafts—The poles attached to a carriage, sleigh, or cart, between which a horse or pony is hitched to pull the vehicle.

Sleigh—A horse-drawn vehicle that has "runners" for gliding over snow or ice instead of wheels.

Slip knot—A type of knot, also known as "quick release," which can be quickly and easily untied in case of a problem, such as the horse or pony falling down or getting hung up.

Soft brush—A brush made for grooming a horse or pony's coat and face; it is the same shape as a hard brush, but has softer, longer, natural bristles.

Spook—An action of the horse or pony in which he shies away nervously from something he is not familiar with.

Stallion—A male horse or pony that has not been neutered and may be used for reproductive purposes.

Star—Any white mark on the forehead of a horse or pony, located above the level of the eyes.

Straw—The material used for bedding in a stall; it consists of stalks of grain from which the grain has been removed and the stalks baled. It should be bright yellow and not dusty.

Tack—Equipment used in riding and driving horses or ponies, such as saddles, bridles, harnesses, etc.

Tack box—A container with a handle used to transport grooming tools, bridles, etc., to horse shows or other events.

Tack trunk—A large trunk usually kept in the stable, which contains the equipment used by the rider, such as as bridles, grooming tools, saddles, lead ropes, medicines, etc.

Throatlatch—The narrow strap of the bridle, which goes under the horse's throat and is used to secure the bridle to the head.

Traces—The thick leather straps on the harness that attach it to the carriage, allowing a horse or pony to pull the vehicle.

Trot—A rapid, two-beat gait in which the front foot and the opposite hind foot take off at the same time and strike the ground simultaneously.

Trough—A long, shallow receptacle used for feeding or watering animals.

Tugs—Common name for the leather straps attaching the shafts to the breeching straps of a horse-drawn vehicle.

Udder—The mammary glands of a cow, where the teats are attached and the milk is produced.

Wash stall—An enclosed area, usually inside the stable, with hot and cold running water, where a horse or pony may be crosstied and bathed.

Whinny—A high-pitched, loud call of the horse.

Winter coat—The longish hair that the horse or pony naturally grows in the winter to protect him from the cold. In the spring, the winter coat "sheds out" and the body becomes sleek again, with a short hair coat.

Withers—The ridge at the base of the neck and between the shoulders of a horse or pony. The saddle sits on the horse's back behind the withers, and we measure the horse or pony's height by measuring from the ground to the top of the withers.

Photo: Christopher Myers

About the Author

A horse lover since early childhood, JoAnn Dawson lives with her husband Ted and their two sons on a horse farm in Maryland, where they operate a bed & breakfast and offer riding lessons, carriage rides, horse shows, and a summer camp. JoAnn teaches Equine Science at a local college and is an actress and animal wrangler for film and television. She has enjoyed competing over the years on her American Paint Horse, Painted Warrior, but it is Butterscotch the pony who accompanies her on school visits and book signings. Butterscotch is so comfortable around kids that he may be the only pony in the country who is allowed to go into classrooms! Learn more about the author and her farm at www.luckyfootseries.com.